Voices fro[illegible]

Ingrid Storholmen was [illegible] on 22 May 1976. She studied literature at the University of Bergen, and spent one year at a creative writing school. She was the literature editor of *Morgenbladet*, a culture newspaper in Norway. For five years, she was the writer-in-residence at 'Adrianstua', a writer's house in Trondheim. She started the Trondheim International Literature Festival during her stay there, and also founded the literary magazine *LUJ* with two colleagues. She has published five books: *The Law of the Poacher* (2001, Shamespeesch); *Graceland* (2005); *Siri's Book* (2007); *Voices from Chernobyl* (2009); *To Praise Love* (2011) published by Aschehoug in Oslo, Norway.

She has received many literary awards and prizes for her work, and her poetry has been translated into eighteen languages. *Voices from Chernobyl* bagged the Sult Prize 2010, and was shortlisted for the 2009 Critics' Prize, the 2009 Brage Award and the 2009 Youth Critics' Prize.

Marietta Taralrud Maddrell (Mira) was born in England in 1943 to a Norwegian father and Swedish mother. She is a wandering ascetic who supports social causes like underprivileged children's education in India, and brings support and succour to those who need her services. She knows many languages like Norwegian, Swedish, Italian, Greek and Hindi. Having spent three years circumambulating the course of the river Narmada on foot, she has written an account of her journey in the book *Narmada Called Me From the Far Himalayas.* Some of her translations from Hindi to English include seminal works on the river Narmada by the noted Hindi and Gujarati writer and environmentalist, Amrit Lal Vegad: *Narmada: River of Beauty* (2008, Penguin India), *Amritsya Narmada and Tire-Tire Narmada* (forthcoming). She took up the translation of this novel in support of the anti-nuclear movement in India and for the exceptional nature of the narrative.

Voices from Chernobyl

INGRID STORHOLMEN

Translated from the Norwegian by
Marietta Taralrud Maddrell

HARPER  PERENNIAL

NEW YORK • LONDON • TORONTO • SYDNEY • NEW DELHI • AUCKLAND

First published in India in 2013 by Harper Perennial
An imprint of HarperCollins *Publishers*
A-75, Sector 57, Noida, Uttar Pradesh 201301, India
www.harpercollins.co.in

First published in Norway in 2009 as *Tsjernobylfortellinger* by Aschehoug

2 4 6 8 10 9 7 5 3

This translation has been published with financial support from NORLA
(Norwegian Literature Abroad)

P-ISBN: 978-93-5029-587-8
E-ISBN: 978-93-5029-969-2

Typeset in 10.5/14 Berthod Baskerville
Jojy Philip New Delhi 110 015

Printed and bound at
Saurabh Printers Pvt.Ltd.

PART 1

Nuclear energy is the hubris of humanity,
like aspiring to fry bacon on the sun.

On Saturday, 26 April 1986 at 01.23 a.m., something went horribly wrong with Reactor Four at the Chernobyl Nuclear Power Station in Ukraine. An experiment to produce electricity from the residual energy in the steam generator was on, and several precautionary guards were down then. Uncontrollable heat was produced in the process, which brought on an explosion of steam in the core of the reactor. The explosion blew away the reactor's roof and the graphite in the core caught fire. The blaze lasted for several days, casting huge quantities of radioactivity a thousand metres up into the atmosphere. To quench the fire, five thousand tonnes of lead and stones were air-dropped from helicopters. It was a long time before the local people were given warning and evacuated. Later a concrete sarcophagus was built around the reactor, and a zone 30 kilometres around the power plant was cordoned off; nobody was allowed to stay within that circle.

It is an evening in spring, the air is mellow. Some people are getting ready to go on the night shift, others are enjoying the warm evening – one to hang out with sweethearts.

The child likes the word 'atom'. I explain that it is both big and small. At the same time? asks the child. Yes, I reply. The river Pripjat is wide and yellow. The child wants us to go there. Can't we play war with the atoms? No, the atom is our worker, not our soldier, they said, I say. It is the weekend and I am uneasy. Something must have happened at the plant last night. Something bad… I can almost feel it in my bones.

We saw trucks and overcrowded buses leaving Pripjat. This was where all the workers at the plant lived. We began to realize that something serious had happened.

The children came home from school, they had been told to change their clothes and stay indoors. People started hoarding food. I remember I peered over in the direction of the plant. There was a thick haze, the chimneys seemed to vanish into the sky. When I got home, my husband was already there; they had been ordered to evacuate the village.

We weren't allowed to take anything with us, neither Nataliya's puppy nor Alexei's trombone. The children cried. The youngest one put his teddy in a bag. I phoned my uncle. He is a farmer and didn't want to abandon the cows and the newly-sown fields. The soldiers who fetched us knew nothing. We asked when we could come back, but they only shook their heads. First we were driven to Kiev, and from there we had to go further by train. There was a crowd, but we who were coming from Chernobyl were allowed on first. Nobody wanted to sit near us.

The roads are gravelled, hard compressed; no dust flies up even when they are dry. My skin prickles, as if it senses radiation. My hand goes automatically to my throat and feels my thyroid gland move up and down.

The black spots on my skin grow bigger. Now they are as big as coins. Mother's spots are even bigger, and her hair is beginning to fall out. I know she is going to die.

The children were told to draw what had happened. Many drew the sky with flames, others drew abandoned blocks of flats. One girl, I remember, drew a deer going round in circles in a black field.

How could we believe what they said. That we only had to wash our hands. We didn't want to understand. The tomatoes grew bigger that year, and cucumbers and cabbages too. A little radiation promotes growth, but it is dangerous to eat them just the same.

Don't think too much, that's what's dangerous. If you start thinking, you're lost. Work, as much as possible. Let go, see things change, understand how they change – the smell inside your work gloves, sweat from other days. Go on working, go on, and the days then go on by themselves. Of course, they do.

We were ordered to shoot the dogs. We were hunters, used to killing wild animals, but not pets, cats and puppies who came and licked our hands. All of them had to be shot, shot and buried.

A photograph shows twenty-three men in front of the sarcophagus they are building to stop the radioactive leakage from the reactor. The men's face masks are hanging under their chins, they are smiling and holding up a placard between them that says *Morituri te salutant!* Those who will die, salute you!

Those who saved us smile. Not yet branded with death, they smile and wave. Now their names are in Vladimir's book. He is keeping a register of his workmates. He has a system: those who are entered in blue are sick, those in red are invalid, and those who are recorded in black are no longer living. Their dates appear in columns: born 1947, died 1987; born 1939, died 1991; born 1953, died 1999. They looked for volunteers to dive down into the heavy water to open the hatch under the reactor. Swimming in heavy water amounts to suicide, but they had got a lot of volunteers.

There is supposed to be a golden fish in the river Pripjat. Many people have seen it. They say you can see it gleaming in the depths. The children say it has swum in the heavy water, that they want to try it too: Maybe we will become golden children, they giggle. More and more people go there in the afternoons and evenings. Boys bunk school and go there with their flashlights to spear the fish. The river becomes narrower on the way down, but it looks beautiful when it widens out again. Fishing is not allowed here any more. The waste from the reactor fire had poured straight into the river. Yet nobody wants to miss the hunt for the golden fish.

Light shines in your eyes – is this your dream? You lean out over the bank. There might be a lot of golden fish in there.

The reactor is no more dangerous than an illicit domestic distiller.

Acute Radiation Syndrome

If too many of the body cells die, we get an acute condition of illness called the Acute Radiation Syndrome. The symptoms of this illness vary, depending on the tissues affected. Tissues with frequent cell division are more sensitive than tissues whose cells divide slowly. Therefore, in adults, blood-forming tissues (stem cells in the bone marrow), the lining of the intestines and fertility cells are very sensitive to radiation, while skin and mucous membranes, lungs and muscles are less sensitive, as also bone, cartilage and nerve cells. Foetuses and children in a stage of rapid growth are particularly vulnerable to radiation damage.

Vitya has been looking at it for maybe three seconds before he realizes it's the alarm flashing. Something has gone wrong with the test, and the director has gone home! He removes the tube to set off the alarm system. The other reactors must be closed down. For an instant, he hesitates before he hits the main alarm code and the danger code. What's happening, why can't he see anything? Maybe it is not true. Maybe he is losing it, just when he is about to get a medal. But he heard the bang, just now. It was as if the whole roof blew off. It could be a matter of life and death for the boys inside, and himself. Suddenly it hurts to breathe, and there's a foul taste far in on the tongue, the taste of copper, maybe. Now I won't have to paint banners for the First of May parade... How stupid it is to think like that. A man comes in, so blackened and burnt that he can't recognize him by anything but his voice; it is the head of Reactor Number Four.

Have you phoned Fire and Ambulance? Idiot! I'll get you impeached. People are dying in there. Get them to call in firemen from the whole district. The same goes for doctors and nurses. I'm going out to hang myself. I have uranium in my hair, that white lump there... This is the worst thing I have ever seen. And it's Number Four that was as gentle as a wagtail in spring. It's the director's fault, this experiment. After you've sounded the alarms, ring my Lena, say she must close the window where the kids are sleeping and they mustn't go out. Say I loved them. He hurries out and shouts in the passage that the electricity is out, but he knows these corridors better than the redcurrant garden at home.

The fire station answers. Vitya can hear the laughter in the background cut off abruptly. At the hospital, they remind him that everyone must take iodine tablets. They say it is the only thing that counteracts the radioactivity that accumulates in the thyroid gland: Don't be tough guys. Eat them and put on the protective gear. Vitya peeps into the box where the tablets are meant to be. All that's left in there is a half-empty packet, with an expiry date in 1981.

He is sick. Something's wrong with his eyesight, it is not clear. It's blurred, like swimming under water with your eyes open. He must get out but can't remember the way. The ambulance men find him in the chair, curled up, apathetic. Then he vomits in someone's lap, thinks it must stink, but it doesn't. He laughs, hears the nurse, whose lap he has thrown up in, shout: We must hurry, now he is going into the elated phase, now it's urgent. Has anyone spoken to Moscow? We have lots of people we must send there. What are they dawdling about? It's urgent. We must get a special plane. At the hospital, he manages to sit up. He sees people from the shift lying on mattresses on the floor, but not Grigory, his brother's best friend. Nurses run around with iodine tablets for everyone, while the senior doctor scolds. Everyone is pale, some are burnt. Those who are only pale are dealt with first, even if the others have more serious injuries. He throws up again, hears the doctors murmuring to each other that it is better if there is blood, more natural… What is this white sickness?

Give me a mirror. I want to see if I'm alive, see if my breath mists the mirror. Thanks. You are kind. I'll be careful. Ask them to fly a bit slower, it's going too fast and I want to see. Why am I talking so much? It's tiring. I'm not usually like this.

This isn't my face! What's happened to my face? It's quite grey. What has happened to me? Answer. Stop! I want to get out of the plane. Now!

I had just got my promotion, the uniform was brand new. They could afford it then. My wife dreamed about a summer cottage, the girls were six and eight. We were making plans for the First of May celebrations. I wanted to show myself off and had accepted to give the keynote speech in Kiev (just acted a bit unwilling at first, but when the older colonels slapped me on the back and said that's something one has to do well, address people, be calm and methodical, be authoritative, I said yes). We went into the Officers' Mess and drank. We had been sitting there a long time when one of the young lads from the telegraph came running in. We could see there was something wrong with him. We tried to calm him down, offered him a vodka, but he refused, waving a piece of paper at us. REACTOR NUMBER FOUR ON FIRE STOP LARGE QUANTITIES OF RADIOACTIVITY LEAKING OUT STOP WHAT ARE WE TO DO STOP INFORM MOSCOW? STOP

We sobered up that instant, sent the boy away, and decided to have a meeting at Prokorov's office. For God's sake, keep it secret, was the first thing he said. Does anyone know? Have people noticed anything? Find out at once, Ivanov. Are there many dead? Are the firemen in place? Avoid panic! Evacuation? Not yet. We must have more information. Close that damned window, goddammit! What the devil! If we just breathe it in…

I just wanted to get home. I thought about Anna and Anastasia. My wife always let them sleep with the window open. May I phone my wife? The others merely looked at me. Now we must keep our cool here. You are new and have to learn. We were not allowed to leave before we had promised not to say anything, not even to our families. Coming home, I closed the window in the children's room, and peeped down at them where they lay sleeping, with their hair spread out on the pillow, Anna with her thumb in her mouth, still so little. My wife was half-asleep but mumbled something about how late I was, the Officers' Mess had shut long ago, did I have a mistress? I went into the bathroom and showered, washing my hair thoroughly. On the First of May, I gave my speech. Rumours had started going round that Pripjat would be evacuated. I was not to say a word about the accident, lest it should upset people. The boss had ordered me to take the girls with me to the parade: When they see it is safe for your girls to be outdoors, they will be assured that all is well. I took them with me, all dressed up in their new frocks. They smiled and waved at the soldiers and veterans who marched past and at the red flags. I don't remember what I said. Don't remember anything but their smiles. That was when I made up my mind to take them with me to Sweden. I knew about a place on the coast I had been to as a fifteen-year-old for an International Communist Youth rally; I was picked as a representative. I remember the girls there were blonde and really pretty, the countryside was peaceful and green, soothing on the eye. I decided to go there. I couldn't have taken my wife along; everything had to happen without anyone knowing. Else I would have been jailed, and for a long time. I fetched my girls from school in the service car, telling the driver that I wanted to drive myself, that Anastasia had fallen ill and the school had phoned, asking someone to come. All went well. They said nothing at the airport, even though they had been told to be extra vigilant. I put down plenty of banknotes at the barrier. The girls were pleased that they were going on a surprise holiday but confused about why mother wasn't to know anything. When the plane took off, I knew I would never return.

We were brought to the reception, but I noticed that the staff were reluctant. They knew where we came from and were scared. We had to wash ourselves clean, and all our clothes were destroyed. I sat in the hotel and drank. In the evening, some women came into the bar. They sat down, whispered among themselves, and looked at me. They asked if I spoke English, and if I would like to treat them to a drink. I waved them away, but one of them didn't go. She was red-haired, pretty and cheeky. I wanted to screw her. Suddenly I realized that was the only thing I wanted. She looked at me, chattering away without a pause. It was obvious she liked my silence. She asked me if I wore a uniform; I said, yes. She invited me up to her room. We had more drinks. She asked if I was a KGB officer; I said, no. She laughed and asked once again. I grabbed her skirt and pulled it up. She took off her panties and I took her from behind on the table. Are you from the KGB? She asked again while I thrust hard into her. I replied with a new thrust. Say it, she moaned. Yes, I said, I've come straight from Chernobyl… And that made her come.

The girls speak Swedish now, have nearly forgotten Ukraine. I have not. The only way I can return is as a criminal. Under another name, operating in the twilight zone, I could have got to see the lanes of Podill again. My parents, I don't know how they are. My wife, she must hate me. I have a hole in my back, I have had it ever since I left, a huge hole through which the air seeps in and out. It doesn't show though. The girls don't know about it. They stopped asking about their mother quite soon. They realized that something was terribly wrong but accepted that they had to live here. They are ordinary Swedish youngsters now, with a school life and boyfriends, but Anna also has a bit of a hole in her back. Now and then I see she can't manage to keep control of her face. Maybe it was the departure, its insecurity – will he make us move again?

But they know that I saved them. They have read about the accident, talked about it. Anna looks at me: How could you not say anything to the other children, the young mothers with baby buggies who stood watching the parade? How could I have? I saved my own but said nothing to my sisters, to the neighbour or the others. I punish myself by not drinking, by not allowing myself to forget. I see my wife in Anna. There's something about the cheeks, the arch of her eyebrows... She was never my great love, but Valentina deserved to know that her daughters are alive.

I drive a taxi in Stockholm, we moved there after a few years. We are called the Bengtsons now: Victor, Anne-Stina and Anna Bengtson. They have not found me yet. You get plenty of time to think in the taxi at times. More and more often, I long to phone my sister, a thought that has been suppressed for several years. And every evening I follow the weather forecast for Kiev; tomorrow it will be 27 degrees. Here, just by the Old Town, it is 14 degrees. In Kiev we would have gone down to the river on an evening like this at the end of April. Yes, the anniversary is approaching. That must be why I am all the more thoughtful. Mother, maybe she died because we went away... But I saved my children. I would do it again. A Party loyalist, I simply let myself be sucked in – oops! I had a promotion, and then, I was caught.

Now the government is called something else, but no doubt the old guys at the top are safe in their seats. A system that needs heroes must have bad guys too; I will always be on that list. Suddenly Anna comes and knocks on the taxi window: Father, I saw it was you. Can you drive me home, I forgot my jacket at Kerstin's house? Just as she closes the door, she pinches her finger and swears in Ukrainian. I jump, can hardly get the car to start. Always something or another, one day it is sure to go wrong. The hole in my back will grow until I disappear completely. Anna looks at me. There is an accusation somewhere in her eyes. I switch on the radio. The weather forecast is over. When she jumps out at our house, there is a slip of paper left behind on the seat where she was sitting: Valentina, and the phone number I still remember, + 410 – 58 – 96.

I have seen burns patients for twenty years, but those we took in that night were different. It was something to do with their skin colour. Their body organs had imploded, and the result was a little shadow on a piece of skin on the upper arm. We knew that the stretcher-bearers who brought them in were sacrificing their lives; maybe they knew it themselves. It is strange how closely we have lived from, and around, the power plant, and so few of us knew anything about radioactivity, nuclear physics and the dangers of radiation. Had we known, would we have lived here, would the housewives have dared to send the children out, air clothes on the balcony, sow pumpkins, kiss their husbands 'good night shift', and simply gone to bed? Humanity needs a hole in the sand to hide its head in. Several psychologists would like to get to the bottom of protective mechanisms, repressions and the whole subconscious. I think about how wrong that is. Subconscious processes are formed precisely because we need them. I have respect for unconscious mechanisms. If you take them away, we cannot call anything normal any more. Do you hear the sirens? They have gone away near the Culture Institute now. I have never got used to the sirens coming close. I was in Afghanistan, the sound of the sirens there was different, but it gave me the same feeling.

One night I was woken up by someone's breath in my ear. I thought it must be soldiers and opened my mouth to scream, but I got a kiss instead of a blow, and two delicate little hands pulled me up. It was a woman. She couldn't manage to say what the matter was. I saw it. She was pregnant. Certainly with one of our men. She wanted me to take it out. It could have been me, I remember thinking while I fetched the curette and the suction equipment. That was the worst assignment in the whole war. It was like that here, too, after the accident. I don't know how many children were born here in 1986, but it was not a big batch. Some speak of 200,000 abortions in Belarus. I scraped and scraped. We were never able to find out if it was right, whether it was really necessary. We couldn't tell which ones would have been healthy, running around or poring over a math lesson now. We live in the Middle Ages, the time in the middle, between two ages – after the emission and before the isotopes have gone.

Sounds in a hospital at night. Far away a door closes, it's so quiet that you can hear it. The pressure in the vein that has the intravenous drip inserted is too much. The vein feels so small, you think it will burst. The ambulance drives out and comes back. You begin to think about the twins, one big and the other small, without eyes. You have to look out of the window. There's darkness and yellow lights. You see two big chimneys, steam and smoke puffing out of them. You begin to sense a smell, see in front of you amputated body parts – hands, feet with gangrene, ears, wombs, abortions, the smoke of foetuses. You get out of the bed, take the intravenous drip tube and the stand with you. The old woman you share the room with is asleep at last, after coughing and muttering prayers all night. Maybe they were not prayers, maybe she was talking to someone, a faint stream of whispers, but with pauses, as if answers came from somewhere, maybe from her dead husband, or Christ, or from herself. You must go away, open the door and feel the good draught against the legs that have lain under a quilt for several weeks now. You are not dizzy and know where to go, downwards, towards the basement where there's a lift. You drop four storeys and open the door. There are more passages to go through before you get to the autopsy tables. You just want to lie down a little and rest.

Speak to me!

Wake, something in between the lips. When you notice the thirst, the lips, greedier than an infant, have completely sucked it into themselves. Juice, thin, thin juice. Before you have managed to swallow anything, the damp cotton wool stick is taken away. Anger makes you open your eyes. Your lips cling to the pale pink cotton wool stick again on its way into your mouth, suck and bite hard into it. No, says a voice, don't drink, you will only throw up. I will just moisten your mouth a little. Yes, like that. You must not try to sit up, you have just had an operation. Think of your wounds. They'll grow bigger. Be quiet. Yes, I know you are thirsty again, but then you must promise me not to suck.

The ceiling light is so bright!

My son. Have you seen him? He must be lying in this hospital. I must go in. He is calling for me. I know you know something about him. He is only a little hurt. Maybe in his leg. Hey, answer me. Have you seen someone with red hair? Not all that red. Maybe the fire took away his hair. No. It didn't. I'm waiting here. Don't come with that death certificate again. It's not him. There are many people who are called Yuri. Many people were named that after Gagarin, his namesake. You understand? I'll wait a bit longer. May I be allowed in? Are you asking me to go? Where shall I go when he is here? Was I here yesterday? It is today I am searching. I've brought chocolates. What is long ago? The accident? It's today I'm searching. I'm searching now. Can you see him inside from behind the windowpane. You are not looking. I can see you are not looking. Let me see. Just a bit. I am quite clean. Had a bath yesterday and wore fresh clothes. Are you laughing? My son is calling. I'm not crying. You can't refuse. The certificate is fake. The papers are fake. Are you tired? Many people who ask. I must also be allowed to ask. I won't go. Shall I bring something for you? Jam. It is good jam. No, not from the zone. Are you looking at me? I won't go. The certificate is fake. I don't want to see it. I got one in the post. It wasn't long ago. The fire was yesterday. Smell the smell of singe. What's that you're saying? No. You can take the chocolates. I'll buy more tomorrow. Maybe sweet things are not good for him. Don't push me. I'm standing here. It's my place. Two years. What do you mean? I haven't stood here for two years? I came by bus just now. The new buses come all the way here. That's good. It's a long way to walk otherwise. He will help me around the house. My son is calling. Hear his voice. Here. Here I am. I'm coming. I'm coming at once. Guards. Why do you have guards? Don't push me, I said. I won't go. He is calling. Calling!

The child is screaming! Today he is a wolf. The wolf seizes the sun and gobbles it up greedily. The sun goes down inside the wolf's stomach. The child is afraid of the dark, some rays come out of his ear. Despite that it has become cold and dark. The child struggles. He sends out rays through his mouth, and that frightens people. The rays are poisonous, they make the skin shrivel up.

The child is screaming! Today he is the rain. The rain is yellow, it sticks to your hair and cannot be washed away on the inside... The child rains. He does not know that he has become dangerous. The rain will not stop being rain. It falls on the birches with new leaves, which shrivel up and become wrinkled, like an old man's skin. The child is not aware of this. It rains just as it always has. Why shouldn't it? The clouds are vapours, the rivers are full of clouds, and there are seeds lying in wait in the ground.

The child is screaming! Today he is the cells, in things that are smaller than little darting tadpoles. He attacks himself. He feels uneasy, as if his body is stuffed with ants and sewn up. He can't scratch himself, the cells are too soft. They live by themselves, they are infected and do not know it. The child cannot but be a child. Nobody can ask him why he cries. He is too big and too small for that. He cannot rely on things being as they were any more. The child is older than himself, but is unaware that he is the beginning of a story.

We carry on as if nothing has happened, carry on with the little things that fill up life. I write my name on everything I come across – books, newspapers, toilet rolls, telephone kiosks. I have to write that I exist. I sit inside the tractor shed all day, not thinking. It is like when you wake up much too early and lie tossing and turning. You don't think proper thoughts, you drift. Increasingly I've stopped thinking. It's easier to let it be, but I drone along steadily like the tractor, as I idled away time as a child. Let the tractor drive on the least amount of fuel, enough to cruise but not enough to power the searchlights. I probe for what I might find in my ears. The tractor is parked by evening. I linger long afterwards. I go into the tractor shed and plough in. I write my name on the tractor roof. Slowly I write it several times, my full name: Kolya Kozlyuk. I hold on tightly. Don't want to be down there in the slag. Kolya Kozlyuk. I write all over the roof. It looks like doodles, my name on the roof of the tractor that buries atoms. You can't use a spade against atoms. You can't use a name against emptiness.

Outside the town, the tractors go back and forth day and night. We are ploughing the whole time. We've been told that it's an important job, that the radioactivity must be removed from the top layer of the soil, and the tractor sheds must be completely airtight: Don't open the window, the dust here is dangerous. We sit there, behind the yellow eyes, which prowl restlessly in the evenings, going back and forth, turning up new stripes of earth. The soil has to be turned. Maybe the underlying layer is not contaminated, maybe all will be well by springtime. I am healthy, but I am ill. To live in this sickness, to take the pain into oneself... It could have been otherwise, we had deserved that, but it was Chernobyl that was hit. I still write my name on the roof inside the tractor shed. Only Kolya, I have to use smaller and smaller letters, for there isn't much space left. When I go for a walk, I see the hunters coming out of the forest. They have caught a boar and are happy, regardless. Everyone wants to eat the meat. There is no choice. No escape, no saving. Only phosphorescent ghosts and hourglasses.

It will soon be autumn, the forest is full of elk. But it is still not permitted to eat their meat. To follow a new spoor, follow the tracks all day, until just before it is too dark to shoot. The bull elk stands there, broadside on to the hunter, as if it is waiting for the bullet. It runs, it falls, kicks its legs convulsively and becomes still. Then you can go close and shoot a bullet into its head. You never forget the first animal you kill, said the old folk, you never forget the taste of warm blood, the strength in it. Just after the accident, he found a baby in the forest while he was hunting. It was a newborn baby, a boy, only some hours old. He took the baby all the way to the hospital. They took it in, but he knows what to expect when the infant becomes big enough. It will be transferred to the children's department of the mental hospital, never to come out again; nothing penetrates there, neither the light of the sun nor its warmth, not a toy, nor a friendly hand. Dying when nobody knows about it, does that amount to dying?

⚬

The old man goes around, saying goodbye to his apple trees, and to the little outhouse. He built it himself, like everything else here. He weeps and is not afraid to show it. He talks with his neighbours, thanks them, and says he hopes they will be his neighbours in the place he is moved to.

A life in an apple tree, planted and harvested, played around and climbed in. His wife used to stand under the apple trees and cover herself with spring. They made love when she came in, white petals fell off her person into the bed and onto the floor. It was their own spring sacrifice. She is ill now, can't go out for the farewell. She will not notice that he is doing this for her, but he is. They are being evacuated three years too late. She is ill and will move only to die. The children had been asking them to leave for a long time, he knows, but here he had enough food for himself and his wife. Now he will get 'charity money', not enough to live on. The dahlias will flower for themselves now, nobody will wonder what colour they will be.

PART 2

The boar yawns, exposing a gullet that looks like ours. The second piglet disappeared into the darkness of its throat. The sow gave birth several days before her time. He should have removed the boar from there earlier. The sight of that blood... He has seen worse things, but even so it shouldn't have happened. Every piglet is needed. There is so little food in the market, people buy without asking where the meat comes from. They were never evacuated. The soldiers came, but he had already sown and did not want to go. He and his wife stayed. Maybe that was wrong. The isolation has not been good for her. She is always lying on the floor when he comes in. He sees her taste the curtains. She wants him all the time. He has to taste her, lick the fingers she hides inside herself. He doesn't want to, but it calms her. She sings wordlessly. It is not his wife singing, it's the boar. The boar howls when he has eaten the piglets. He is still hungry. His wife smacks her lips. She caresses the boar when she comes into the warm barn. Steam rises from anybody who comes in from outside. It is winter now, the warmth of the animals helps, for it is colder indoors on the floor. He must steal more firewood from the forest behind the house, the owners are gone. Gusts of wind moan, sweeping over the plains. It doesn't help to close the windows, the wind finds loopholes through the curtains that are still damp. He goes out and stays there for as long as possible. His eyes can't see properly in the dark. Taking up a different tool each time, he always finds something to do, otherwise something in him cracks. The plough is not sharp, it can be sharpened; that will use up the evening. He can wait until she falls asleep, but she doesn't sleep. She lies wide awake and complaining – her tongue can't taste, it has become cork or leather, it rasps. She howls a boar's howl. He knows he strikes, strikes where there can be no speaking. In the barn, the sow and boar are family. Spit has no colour, unlike blood. It must be quiet now, the ear has withdrawn into the head. It has heard enough for the time. And the boar is quiet without an audience. God takes care that the children don't come visiting us, it is dangerous now. They are in Kiev and come here no more.

The wind blows, but now there are no ears to hear, no ears, no taste. The boar has been stabbed in the throat, its legs thrash about for a long time afterwards, running away in the air. The slaughtered beast must hang and become tender. It looks like a man, just as tall.

Boar soup is not tasty. His wife tastes the tongue, pale and white, bloodless. She kisses the pig's snout. Maybe it tastes salty. She drops it to the floor, and then drops down to the floor herself. He will not go in. He will not do that. He will not go until the soup is cooked. Once the soup is ready, he will go in and eat. It is colder in the barn, she won't go there again. She won't go to Kiev. She will stay. She doesn't lick the curtains so often now. They will not get a new boar. He sharpens the plough thoroughly. There's a lot of work that can be done, like picking up windfall apples. She rinses the apples well, removes the maggots. Soon it will be time for apple soup.

Irina has not slept since the accident a hundred nights ago. She is going to move tonight. But when she gets to the door, she finds the door locked, from the inside and from the outside. Then she understands that she has to stay anyway. On the hundred and first night, she makes up her mind to stop biting her nails, for they have become poisonous, and she lies down to sleep, even if she is radioactive. The coal has used itself up, there is no more available. I look like a ghost, thinks Irina and eats pickled gherkins, crying to herself.

She talks to the priest. He is of the view that there is some sense in Chernobyl being warmed by an internal reactor. Irina decides it is right and does not light a fire all winter. In February, Raisa comes and finds her lying in bed, wrapped up in layers and layers of rugs. Like a flower with large eyes, thinks Raisa and fetches coal for Irina.

Raisa writes down her dreams in the red book. She does this every morning, shaking her head. One night she dreamed she was a big, fat, cured ham, which was sent round the world to be eaten. A large piece fetched up in Rome, another landed in Sweden, a small piece in Romania. She remembered that the ham had thoughts and feelings, that it had been more unpleasant to be sliced when it was her father and mother who were going to help themselves to her. Raisa does not understand that dream, it is not like anything she has dreamed before. The following night, Raisa dreams that she is a chick enclosed in an egg. Raisa-chick lies in the egg, feeling that it is good to be yellow surrounded by white. Raisa wakes up shouting: I don't want to hatch, I don't want to hatch. Afraid, she runs over to Yevgeni, wearing only her dressing gown. He is painting on a large canvas. A small person playing a violin inside the nucleus of an atom. Yevgeni was called to the roof of the reactor to shovel away lumps of uranium. Yevgeni could not bear it. He has become an old man, although he is only thirty-five. He is waiting for the baker's to open. He has been eating cigarettes since four this morning and is quite green. He does not dream. He thinks that his ability to dream was blasted to bits. He himself used a spade against the atoms. I buried earth in the earth, thinks Yevgeni. I will paint that, an earth that can't bear itself. I'll paint all night because the day is not enough.

Raisa puts salt under her pillow. She puts feathers under her pillow. When she tries soil, her dreams get more violent than ever. Raisa dares not sleep, but she does not dare to stop dreaming either. She understands that the police have planted those dreams because she may report what she knows about the experiment at the plant. Can anxiety be untangled from the nightmare?

Irina glows. She had forgotten what it was like to be warm. Now she can feel the sun under her feet. The fire pursues me, the sun under my feet is fire. I move my teacups and nobody notices. Let me move the potted azalea and the picture of auntie. But when Irina is about to carry the picture out under her coat, she finds that the door is locked. The zone will not let me escape, thinks Irina and digs herself in for yet another winter.

The piano has to stand in the cellar. Ivan can't play it after the accident. His hands no longer have the right touch; he cannot cope with the sound of his own playing. Six men carry it down. Every day he goes and looks at it, dusts the keys; his fingers obey him that much. Later, they just hang down slackly and are not able to grasp anything, not even able to stroke the piano or help his wife with the firewood. The woodpile looks like half-sized people. Ivan sees how they shrink into cripples when they burn, and knows he must either sell the piano or burn it.

His wife thinks it was because they sold the piano that he got epilepsy. Now he has a seizure nearly every day. The clairvoyant who lives across the street has begun looking closely at him, he can feel it. Ivan wants to drink salt water and feel what it is like to drown.

It is Raisa who has bought the piano. She has dreamed of a piano tuner three nights running, that he sits in her living room, searching for the right notes. She herself will not be able to play the right notes. They will not be harmonies and chords. She puts up a card advertising for a piano tuner, but nobody calls. She waits, knowing someone will come someday. It happens. A man with a hat on his head rings the doorbell. He moves right in and stays on. He sits at the piano, but does not tune it. Maybe he does not know how to, thinks Raisa. Maybe he is from the secret police, come to find out what I know, what my husband told me about the experiment before he died. Raisa makes up her mind to pretend to know nothing, say nothing about the suspicion, say nothing at all, and wait until the stranger speaks. She dreams no dreams while he lives there, and sleeps a black sleep. This is either a good or a bad omen, thinks Raisa. Maybe my dreams have come to an end. She gives the piano tuner sandwiches and sits over the samovar. It will be interesting to see which of us will give way first, she thinks, as if it were a competition. He kisses her. It is a kiss from an old book. Outside in the street, Ivan stands listening for the sounds of his piano.

Irina hears sounds, noises of things exploding and children crying. I can't stand it any more. Now I'm going to move, nobody can really stop me. I will not stay near Chernobyl. I want to live where everything isn't poisonous and spoilt. Irina packs only the bare essentials, without much thought. The icon pictures and plum jam are left behind. She sneaks towards the door at two o'clock; it is darkest then. The door is open now. Irina can't believe she can go wherever she likes. She hurries outside. There is nobody in the streets. She walks and walks. She comes all the way to the station, but it is closed. She thinks she will wait for the first train at four o'clock. She waits, but no train arrives. Now it is nine o'clock. There should have been a train long ago. However, there are no people on the station. There will not be any trains any more.

Raisa dreams again. A piece of wood is burning under water. The deeper it sinks, the more the wood burns. Raisa sees summer birds, while it is autumn now. Outside the house, a telephone is ringing. Raisa dare not peep out. She knows there is no telephone there, someone wants something from her. She does not go out. The telephone keeps ringing, but the summer birds are not bothered. The berry bushes have lost all their leaves, the berries swing on bare twigs. Children stand in the street singing:

> *In Moscow sits the big father,*
> *While we must drink Chernobyl water*
> *Hey ha, hey ha, Chernobyl water.*
>
> *The zone's not closed with wall or door,*
> *Outside the becquerel flows as before*
> *The kids are first to bleed, to sore.*

Raisa wants to write songs about the birds, which crash into car windscreens because they can't live here. People burn the dead wagtails in barrels, it takes a lot of petrol.

Raisa jumps along the road, jumps over all the snails. Just the same, her foot feels like she has hit some, and she slips. The foot turns violet even as she is looking at it. She needs to go to the doctor, but the doctor only cares about the Chernobyl-afflicted. Raisa's foot will have to stay violet. Then she dreams that she is violet all over, that she is a violet scarecrow, which eats all the singing children in town. She eats those who sing the most; they taste the best of all.

Raisa cries in her sleep. She kills children in her sleep and cries. Raisa thought the police were dangerous. Now she has become dangerous herself. She cuts her violet foot with a razor blade and begins to dream mother-of-pearl dreams. When she wakes up, she fills out forms and more forms and registrations, until she forgets the foot and the children but not the dreams. Raisa is larger than her dreams, she is wide awake. She often thinks about the accident. She thinks about her husband who died there. He had told her exactly how they were going to test Reactor Four. It is dangerous to know too much, thinks Raisa. The piano tuner may be a policeman, but until he gives himself away, it is good to have him around. He makes good pâté, and he tickles my ear with his moustache. And when he does that, I laugh, which I never do in my dreams.

Yevgeni takes off all his clothes, puts them in front of his door, and paints naked. He has finished painting pain. Now he wants to express positive things, he just needs to find a form different from before the accident. Humanity lives in suffering. He wants to paint hope. He paints colours separately and colours on top of each other. Strong colours, but not poison yellow or soot black. Yevgeni is happy, aged and naked and happy.

We go on being human after this, thinks Yevgeni... We are always human, and humanity cannot only be in pain. I paint mauve and orange, lines in red and black, and then blue, blue and grey vodka. He paints people on high poles, people stretching themselves. We lift ourselves up... Chernobyl is not stronger than the life force or the sleep that heals. The children will notice laughter in the streets; the sun is not poisonous, even if we believe it is. Naked, he can paint everything. Without ornamentation, the beautiful is most beautiful, thinks Yevgeni. I'll paint until they carry me out. I'll whistle in the coffin. I am bigger than my pain.

Think of old Vadim who walked from here to the Czar in St. Petersburg when injustice had been done to him. Twice he walked the whole way. There and back. Because he believed in justice. We continue to live, this is our justice. How many times can the same person be killed?

Raisa comes in, stepping over the pile of clothes by the door. Seeing the naked man and the new paintings, she is filled with fear. Raisa does not dream any more. She sleeps, without dreams or rest. The sleep is merely a void to pass the night in. Raisa has a sister in Estonia. I should have gone to her, thinks Raisa. When I think about it, I don't understand why I didn't go. I'm scared. Fear is a clingy animal, a grub that fastens itself to the hair and to the hands and clothes, and suddenly you see it creeping round onto your face. Raisa cannot keep going. She has stopped talking to people. It took a while before Irina noticed it, now everyone notices it. Raisa has become silent, so has the piano tuner. She is getting thinner. Thinning to a little line on the road, a twig that stretches forth to bend in the wind. Raisa stops trying. Then the dreams come – they are alive. She dreams that she is dying. Death is a white bubble.

The piano tuner burns his condoms in the stove. They crackle. Sentimentally he says goodbye to all the little Viktors. Thinks about the born children who cry. He has come away from a child. Tatiana, four years old and in the final stage of leukaemia. He abandoned her when she said 'Father, it's so painful. Kill me instead.' He went out along the roads and worked whatever he was needed as: herdsman, waiter, farrier, piano tuner. He does not know whether the girl is still alive, does not want to know. He will never go back. And now, Raisa has started getting thinner as well. She has begun reading the *Bible*. She reads aloud to him from *Revelation*:

> *And the third angel sounded, and there fell a great star from heaven,*
> *burning as it were a lamp, and it fell upon the third part of the rivers,*
> *and upon the fountains of waters, and the name of the star is called Wormwood.*
> *And the third part of the waters became wormwood; and many men died of the waters, because they were made bitter.*

Even though he is from Belarus himself, he knows that the Ukrainian word for 'wormwood' is Chernobyl.

Why does Nature teach us a language she does not understand herself?

MUTATION

There are two kinds of mutation. Gene mutations are changes, which take place in the DNA molecule; they are also called nucleus mutations. The most common nucleus mutation after ionizing radiation is double or single chain breakage, cross-linkaging between the nitrogen base thyamine, or exchange of nitrogen bases. Chromosome mutations are changes in the chromosomes themselves. Such chromosomal alterations can be caused by radiation. While gene mutations involve changes in the inherited information, which is tied to the gene, chromosomal changes involve loss, doubling or changing of whole chromosomes or large parts of the them. These chromosomal defects are produced by ionized radiation until the chromosomes break.

Wormwood grows along the roadside. She throws up on every second plant. It's early in the morning. She should have taken the shortcut through the park. But now she is so tired she does not look out at the crossing, and as cars hoot at her, she clutches her stomach. She is scared he will notice her nausea. Will he hit her? Or maybe cry? Grigori was up on the roof of the reactor. As soon as they met, he told her, this is not forever, this is not marriage, and children – never ever. He was careful, always sent the cold semen out over her stomach, embracing her gingerly. She wanted to know the spasm, hug tightly, like morse. He is going to want an abortion, she knows she can't do it. She sees the child in front of her, thinks about names. Grigori asks outright, she denies it. I must save it, save myself. She kneels on the cement-hard bathroom floor and searches. There, half-wet and crumpled up, are her sister's light blue panties, with spots of blood all over them. Some of those spots have small rust-coloured lumps. They smell different from hers. She wraps the panties in plastic and sends them to him.

Tongue far inside the most open lips, her largest mouth, the kisses don't stretch far enough. She lets out an agitated groan, her hands clutch my shoulders, my hair. No, I can't do it. I won't be able to hold back either. My semen is phosphorescent. The doctor's face appears in front of my eyes. Grigori, you must not… promise me… mutations… monsters. Goddammit! A woman who gets you inside her,

44

lies with an atomic weapon, a deadly nuclear missile. I laugh hysterically, put all the fingers of my left hand inside her. The right hand gropes for her throat, something to squeeze to bits.

I can't see my feet. I am standing upright and can only see a big, big belly, elliptic in shape, and agitated – the baby may come out soon. I have felt the fists boxing against my skin for days. It keeps boxing and boxing, perhaps in anger. Or is the baby trying to tell me something? I have borrowed a larger dress from my sister. She won't have any more now, she says sadly – not after the accident. She isn't trying to scare me because she doesn't know how afraid I am about the knowledge that something is wrong, that there is too much life, not too little, which I was uneasy about at the beginning. My belly is red and huge and abnormal, with all the boxing and the energy. But it isn't twins. Grumbling all the time, I push away Anatoly's hands that want to stroke my belly, press against the pressure from inside and measure, to tell that he exists. I push him away. We should have waited, we knew what we were doing. We had seen deformities, heard of children who were born without a head. We tried just the same. In my dream, the walls are rust-coloured. I lie, looking up at the roof of the cave. At the stalactites dripping down on me at irregular intervals. Drip, wait, drip, drip, long wait, splash. Then, something tears. A waterfall, it originates from me. The water has broken. The floor becomes wet. I am alone, but I am quite calm. My belly sinks. I can see it move downwards. Like a snake that has swallowed a rat, the belly ripples downwards. The water is gone. I drip and create new stones, points that turn upwards. It will be painful for the next person who lies here. I

46

believe I scream, but I am dreaming, so I don't know whether the scream can be heard. I don't push, something pushes itself forward and presses downwards... Two hands grab hold of the stalagmite tips and something hauls itself out – a long, slender, dark body. I don't think. I raise myself up again. The body is still stuck inside me. A face comes up between the shoulders, turned towards me. It has long black hair, and an expression that I have only seen on the faces of very old people. I scream – now I know I am screaming. But the baby just looks calmly at me, takes a new grip on the stalagmite, pulls itself right out of me and falls lightly onto the floor. The dream becomes darker. I can hardly take a glimpse of the shape beside me on the floor – not a sound, not a whimper, nothing. Had it not been for the way it looks at me, I would not have believed it was alive. Can one love a mutant? Now and then drips fall on my forehead. It's chilling but not frightening when you don't think about it. I raise myself up on my elbows and turn over on my side. My eyes start from below, seeing the toes, the thighs, the strong, long stomach with the cord, the chain – we are bound together by a chain. Something or the other stirs in my throat. The lower part of the baby's chest lifts, it breathes, the hands box... And then I see it – between the shoulders near the heart, there is a third arm, with fingers. Three hands! The two normal hands go on thrashing about, the third one stretches and grabs hold of me.

I am not awake yet, I dare not. But we make a pact, I and that outstretched hand: the next time, I will grasp it, hold it.

Autumn rain is heavier than other rain, stringy, like twigs against the face. It is not evening, only dark. Two gravediggers are trying to level the bottom of the hole. The grave is deeper than usual. They say they have orders from the highest quarter to dig them so, for it is a radiation victim who is going into the ground. One of the gravediggers swears because they don't get paid extra for digging deeper graves, and he laughs because it is a stupid idea, this digging deeper – who will the corpse be dangerous for? The dead maybe.

So typical to die this way. Just because he was a hero. A fireman, he became a vegetable, quite quickly so – couldn't bear so much. It's only us lot who drudge all the time, the toughest jobs fall to those who can manage them. Anyone can douse a fire, can't they, Fyodor? Fyodor gives no reply. Without their noticing it, the rain muffles all sound. A woman, about twenty-five, stands at the side of the grave. She stands so close that the tips of her little shoes stick out over the hole. She rocks back and forth without noticing them. But, lady, you must not stand like that, you may fall in. The other gravedigger tries moving closer to her to take her away. Fyodor sees that it is the fireman's fiancée, a widow without rights, as they are called. She stands like a sleepwalker, not crying, just rocking, very slowly and in a controlled manner. Then suddenly, she says: Have you found Yorick's skull?

Wedding dresses are on display. I talk to the dummy in the window. I tell it that yesterday was the first anniversary of the day we should have been married. I have not advertised my dress yet, even though I can't afford to keep it. Nor do I want to. I never open the cupboard where it is hanging, but I see the announcement in front of me: 'Unused wedding dress for sale'. He died during the time we should have been honeymooning in Crimea. He was so ill that we couldn't go through with the wedding ceremony. What use would that have been anyway. In the end, he was not even conscious. And I wasn't pregnant. *This* wasn't the man I wanted to marry either – a charred stump, not a man. Not as he had been – blond. He was blond. Just think, he had worked on the oil rigs and earned money. Now he was going to stay here for a while, take on a very risky commission – the kind that was rewarded with a summer cottage, a car, triple pay. I wasn't scared, didn't think anything could happen. I used to stare straight into the flame of the welder's torch, walk down dark streets late at night. I wasn't afraid. And, he was like that, too – immortal. Could never be anything but young. He should have died immediately, should have been spared that interval between life and nothingness. His hands had been burnt away, little stubs left in their place, here toes and there fingers. The face flattened, a bit of the nose remained. Only his voice was just the same. That was what terrified me the most. Behind all that mutilation, he still existed. Everyone insisted that I go ahead with the wedding; there were only ten days left. I was sick. I vomited if anyone so much as lit a match; it was like pressing a button. Luckily, he quickly got worse. The priest said he refused to marry someone who wasn't conscious. Even 'mother-in-law' had to give in. No doubt she wanted to capture me into the family, make me take care of them when they became old. I didn't feel any pity for him. He had gone. It was only his left overs that remained, something I shouldn't have seen. I hoped he would die quickly, before we would have got back from the Crimea. I looked at the nurses who gave him morphine – looked at them, not him. He died. Burial was the custom in his family, but I wanted him to be cremated. To end something that had been started. They thought the idea barbaric.

The wedding dresses in the window... I must have stood here a long time. The dummy looks emptily at me. She looks at the face of a bride who will not be married.

During the funeral, which is without a priest or music, Fyodor stands by himself at a little distance in the graveyard. He helped to carry the coffin down from the truck and will fill in the hole afterwards. Relatives do not help carry it, that has never been the custom here. Fyodor has been promised an extra bottle for the job. Besides he is curious about the woman he saw yesterday. But she is not there, and he feels disappointed. Only the mother and brothers are present. They kiss the body. Its face is quite black, and Fyodor notices that the youngest brother, about twelve or thirteen years old, shrinks back.

He hears a sound coming from behind him, in the old part of the graveyard where there are only thorn trees and the blue and white crosses of the poor. There stands the woman, hidden behind a broad pine trunk. Her gaze flits from the coffin to the hole and from the hole to the coffin. When they begin to lower the coffin, the woman runs straight past Fyodor; he could have stopped her. She runs fast. And either nobody sees her or they stand there paralysed, confronted with something they have not seen before nor understand. The coffin is half-way down, there is still a small gap between it and the edge of the hole, but she manages to squeeze herself down, swiftly, gracefully – thinks Fyodor – and get under the coffin. Those who are busy lowering it are so bewildered that they don't stop, they simply let go of the ropes. When Fyodor steps forward and throws the first spadeful of earth over the lid, then people begin to shout.

PART 3

Water around the legs, feet down in the mud. I don't feel the water, it's only there, in between my legs. Stand in water, simply stand – I will stand like this. It clucks softly around the thighs.

To be a rock, a little cliff water can cluck around… Temperature and time have gone. Hot or cold, long or short cannot be measured. A little speck of rust in a big arch. Don't fall, pitch, stand. Stand here, in the thought. The thought knows that it stands, that it thinks, that there is water around, a lot of water, with a surface that pine needles and sunshine can float upon. The sun warms the neck a bit. It's not dangerous, not so much for one to duck under. It does not smell of smoke. It smells of nothing, like water – the water and the colour of water. Moisture flows with it in the mouth. It is not deep, the water holds and moves. Holds up boats, moves boats, mermaids, fish. It holds me. I stand in water and feel water. A picture shatters in the water and disappears. Then it is there again. The picture has been there the whole time, it is only the current that streams through it. Still water. The entire surface is still, the feet are still, the water is not flowing. The thought thinks the water, the water thinks the thought, swirling. The smell. The smell of smoke. Grey and blue smoke. The lungs are bound, tight. The water strokes over the chest, not inside in the lungs, over, smoothes out, cools, warms. The toes feel the water and the riverbottom, old water in circulation. The shouts. Must hold onto the wet surface, flow, stand and flow, feel the flow. Never saw the flames, only the smoke. Those who saw the fire, saw death. The water cannons were held by people, the water holds people. Waterweed waves, quietly… sees that it waves, waves over, and under water it waves, whispers about fire, whispers away if you like. The smell of smoke sits at the back of the nose, cannot be washed away. I have tried washing, rinsing, flushing away. The smoke sticks fast, has taken hold. The water swirls. The thought thinks water, thinks in water, holds the water tight around the legs, runs away. The thought runs away, it runs into a waterfall, calm, calm in the water, a wooden boat, the feet stand fast and follow the boat. Just as the water gives way gently under the boat, the thought follows the boat. The boat glides, swims, floats and vanishes in the smoke, is swallowed up, extinguished, lost. The smell again, the smell inside the nose. In the black and blue picture. After the eyes open, you see a blue picture, round it the queen of heaven. She is from the icon you have seen in church, over shop doorways, in books. A picture that came to you. It stands fast behind open eyelids. The picture insists that the blue colour is something other than colour. It exists deep inside you. Without you asking for it, the dream carries it forward, not a film but a picture.

Given. Taken.

I have lost my husband.

Two children are on the way home from school. The girl is
bigger and holds her brother tightly by the hand. They walk
faster than me. There's a sky above the sky. I feel a little
echo of joy, the body sends out light from the apertures,
enough for a star. I remember that I leaned towards you,
so close that my head covered the light from the lamp. I
wanted to show you my beams, wanted to show you that I
was shining. I know you cried afterwards, you had wiped
your tears away when you came back, your voice almost
cleared. But the redness in the eyes gave you away. The
water in your eyes, I could have drunk it, but I wasn't able to
see, and took nothing but what you asked me to – it was like
an agreement. You should be able to die in peace. You did
not deceive me that way, I saw what I was able to see. New
tears, quite white. Don't struggle, oppose, or cry out – for me,
it was enough to rest. Rest in it as it was, as we experienced
it. Rage is exploring, to find something to point at. This was
something different – a calm longing, folded in. Memories
are not so important any more. You could have won, it
could have been a lawsuit. Like the sound of the explosion
before the crash, the sound continues. Now comes the bang,
vibrates the glasses on the shelf… The sound continues far
too long afterwards. You had to be allowed to do it the way
you wanted, I never hindered you. That is why I can stay
here. For you let me be, let me warm your feet when we had

gone to bed and you shivered. Under the quilts, everyone's so small. Remember how it was to be covered up, the sounds of evening so different from the morning sounds. I can't protect myself, I couldn't protect you. But you let me warm you... Later, when you had fallen asleep, I fell asleep close to you, felt the friction of the hair on your thigh against my fingers. I dream that we are quarrelling, that I am cross with you, that my voice is harsh, that you have to wait for me when we are going on a journey into the country, that you sit there dressed and ready, and I dawdle, looking for gloves and my scarf, the soft red one I believe you like. I know what it means, what it means in dreams. It does not mean the same thing when I wake up. You slept quietly, you came a long way. That was something I should have learnt from this. I realized that early, otherwise I would have gone. Your breath took in wing beats, you breathed on the unfurling leaves. And I am the one who got to see this. Your death is beautiful among deaths. I think you smile. I will put clusters of candles on your grave. I am not sad but living – I blink and open the window. There will be air to breathe when you come. Come – I won't cry for you, I promise.

I have lost my husband.

Mist lies over the town, there is light in it. A dog has curled up and is sleeping on the road. It is still sleeping when I return. Oak leaves in the park crumble underfoot. I clench the bandaged hand rather tightly and moan, not a loud sound and hardly a grimace. I cough too much at night, the dream is a warning from the queen of heaven I can't get past. The sound of hands, hands that hold the words, mitosis, cancer divisions inside the cell... I can hear it, falling out to a new me.

Carnations wither. The conversations we should have had... I yearn for you! Mother phones and wakes me up, worried. I talk about Othello. He did not trust Desdemona's love, that is why it went so wrong. The third glass of wine and two pills, they get me thinking. The water in circles in the washing, the dirt, the waste from my face, the black make-up spins down to the drain, faster and faster. You are so close to me. I wait by the window – not so many come here any more – wait all the time but can't go out. The work is to wait, the evening is for waiting, waiting a whole evening, a whole day, a whole minute. When I was studying, we played, we drank gin and tonic in the hotel bar. I remember the lift that went up and down, the sound just before it reached a floor. All the time that sound, a rhythm – intoxication has another rhythm. It is so dry and sunny, it could have been spring in November. But I don't let myself get fooled, I feel the leaves crunching underfoot. I must not remember sounds. I think in sounds. I like the sound of pouring liquor best, slow red wine. The rattle of wind between the double-glazed windows, a tiny wind gone astray.

Right here inside the church, frosty smoke escapes from the priest's mouth. There's no smell of incense, but its memory lingers in the heavy red colour of the wall. I am tempted to light all the candles on the globe, but I won't – not before tomorrow. The priest has been with us for a long time now, even though he is young or maybe as old as Jesus, but I know so little about him. He came in the summer after the accident. Something about his expression made me think he had chosen to come here. He lights a candle by the large icon on the west wall, goes two steps back and looks at it. I don't think he has noticed I am here. He breathes heavily, I can hear it over here. I imagine he is sweating, that sweat runs down his face. He is gentle, many in the parish feel he is not strict enough. He does not shout, he does not console either – he is simply here, all the time. I rummage through papers, pretend that I am getting something ready for the Mass. Suddenly he says my name, asks me to come over. He stares fiercely at me, wild and desperate, and asks whether we should pray together, whether I would lead the prayers. I say it is not right, it is he who is the priest. He asks if I doubt it. No, I say. No. Don't you see all the dead? Two new funerals just tomorrow, one of a four-year-old child who died of leukaemia. Yes, I say. Where is God? he asks. God alone knows, I say slowly. I can't bear to look at his eyes, they are full and empty at once. He lets himself fall to the marble tiles and sobs convulsively. I can't find Him in here any more. Wait until God finds you, I say gently, for God pleads our case against ourselves. He still lies there. A body, a beast of burden for a restless soul. He does not look up when I leave. I will never mention this to anyone, and he will not be able to look me in the eye tomorrow. Because he will rise to the occasion, force himself to say something like 'we can look at the moment of death as a high point in our earthly existence'. Tonight he will encounter God. He will pray, keep vigil. To pray is to listen to God. He will reconcile. It will happen. The little coffin feels heavy already. Pray with me. Pray for me as well.

Nadia washes her hair several times a day, it can never be clean enough. Now she has been out in the rain, so she washes it three times.

Several people know the story of the six-year-old boy who ran around the soldiers when they came home from the rescue service, with orders to burn their protective clothing and uniforms. The boy asked if he might have 'one of the caps, which were so tough'. The soldiers said no. One of the men threw his clothes in the rubbish, where the boy found the hard hat and wore it for weeks. Last year he died of a brain tumour.

Nadia washes her hair, her scalp is dry and itchy. Fear has gone into her body. Her neck is as taut as a piano string. She wakes up at two o'clock in the morning. It should not be like this to be young. She had imagined something different. She had imagined quietness, and maybe security too. She is a member of the Environmental Protection Association. They meet in secret, at different places, discuss sending letters to the West about how Nature has gone to war and how scared they are to eat their food. Nadia does not believe in the West. Now and then busloads of western scientists come here. They have dosimeters with them to measure the radiation levels in the toilet, they eat only sealed packets of food they have brought with them, they peer at the sarcophagus, and off they go again, without speaking to anyone. Nadia has made up her mind not to have any children. She has seen too many deformities. She does not want her children to end up among the bodies, looking like embryos, preserved in spirit and displayed in the museum in St. Petersburg.

At the university, she hands out leaflets. That can be dangerous. She is afraid that her mother and grandmother would be punished if they arrest her. She does it anyway, a small defiance against a big machine. A leaflet against radioactive rainfall. Nikolai hands them out with her. He is afraid too. They throw up the canteen food behind the History Department, and hand out some more. Nikolai's father fell out with the Party and was in jail for large parts of Nikolai's growing up. Nadia knows he has forbidden his son to do anything that might court arrest. It is not worth it, says his father. But Nikolai must do something, he can't bear to wait. Nikolai sees all the fatalists, people who don't believe because they don't see. The fatalists are secure. They can't think about the accident if they are to keep on living. Nadia thinks fatalism is death, a death after the Chernobyl death. She and Nikolai hold onto each other. They have begun to receive letters. Every day now, letters arrive in brown envelopes, letters in which they are asked to stop. 'We know about you,' say the letters, 'you might just as well stop.'

Nadia shoves the letters under the bed. They peep out like brown rats, their tails strike the bed when Nadia tries to go to sleep. She meets Nikolai in the woods, they walk under the trees together and dare not speak. The trees are microphones and antennas. Surveillance is like death after Chernobyl.

What is cloud and what is water? The clouds creep down into the water, or maybe the picture is turned upside down. They go out of the town to a rundown farm where a group of old siblings live. Outside stands a car, which belonged to the eldest brother. They did not want to sell it, even though Varslav was the only one with a driving license, and he has been dead for fifteen years. The siblings don't take the leaflets. They smell of mothballs in the doorway. Nadia and Nikolai try another farmer. She works at the nursery. The whole garden is full of silver fir. One can't see the windows. They say she does not have the title deeds for the farm.

Nikolai has half the ring finger missing from his right hand. Nadia has not asked how he lost it, it feels the best of all when the question is inside her. In the city centre, there is a stink of sewage. They hear a wedding procession go past, the whole group smelling of shit.

The day will not end, Nadia waits. She is denied instruction at the university, the teachers do not greet her. She smells of shit. It is raining, and the day contains nothing, nothing to believe in. Then she thinks that maybe it is all wrong... Should she simply live and forget the rest? This is no life. She shits, it runs out of her. Food disgusts the body, the body will not have it. Idleness eats into her head, lumps of snot grow in her mouth. She can't bear to meet Nikolai. She smashes the compass that hangs beside the bed because that too smells of shit. She dreams of torpedoed submarines, men who write letters home just as they are filling up with water. She does not know she is sleeping and that this is a dream. Postcards arrive from friends at the Black Sea. They bathe and talk to each other as usual. The Black Sea is destroyed, but they don't know it. 'Fight the good fight', she thinks, but the good fight is painful. I will turn back to my life, without my life in between. The pictures are bright, braided light. They are also mine, myself with long dusting mops in my ears. The stars have spread themselves out. I could have swum. This is not a reading list, this is grey, good grey. Someone is sleeping in the room, a dark exhalation. I won't breathe any more, I promise. It is going to be brighter now, you will see.

In the sand, there are boots, small tools and other things that people had tried to take with them but had to leave behind during the evacuation. The sand has spread over the remains. The zone is completely deserted. A catastrophe is quickly covered with sand, memory spares the people. Afterwards it was not so dangerous. They laughed at each other as before, ran errands, and made love in narrow beds when the eldest child had fallen asleep. The sand covers Chernobyl. People lie asleep. It is night shift at the plant. Will it go well tonight? It went well last night. It has become routine again. The accident will become like the siege of Stalingrad soon, just something the old folk talk about. The old folk talk for a long time, the wrinkles come out of their faces and down onto the table. There they coil themselves up like rope, with all their smiles and anger and anxieties. It is a strong rope, but nobody wants to use it.

Go out in the zone and fetch firewood, children. Don't lick your fingers, and be quick. Take care that the watchman doesn't see you. And, bring the big logs.

The rope of old age remains lying unused and ageing – the town has moved on. They are old children who run with their backs bent.

Round and round, it rumbles. The large stomach eats, wants more, can take it all. It devours all the new bags that stand on the pavements all along the street, along the rows of blocks of flats. The piles of rubbish become greyer – at last it all becomes whitish – and turn into sludge. The winter says that garbage and gold lie entwined. Here it is hard to understand. In the beginning, carcasses of dogs and cats were heaped up with the rest, and the wheel grabbed and gobbled whatever it might be. I have walked behind the rubbish truck for many years now. The boilersuit is heavy, I have not bothered washing it. I thought that Pushkin was immortal. But for my children, who have to grow up indoors, the poem 'Time of Sadness' does not mean the same thing. We have the books and the fantasies and so much rubbish. I was only going to help out for a month after the accident, and go write the final exam and finish my studies. But I am still here, and I guess I will stay on.

I remember one of the bitches that were thrown into the pit. It wasn't a dog but radioactive rubbish. She clearly had paws, for they stuck out. I thought of Romulus and Remus. Someone must come across us in the forest and found a town here again.

It will soon be empty. The grinder grinds its jaws with nothing in between. There is nothing more to throw in. Actually there is more to throw in, but it is too dangerous to collect it. Atomic waste cannot be ground up and buried. It does not go away like that. Only Stalin would give that famous order: 'Not one step backwards.' Now we have gone many miles backwards – all the way to Chernobyl.

Bethlehem has become old. The shepherds on the ground are filled with days. On the floor in the stable, handheld video cameras whirr, a film rewinds. The flash makes the eyes red. You have to tolerate the 'oh-my-god!' Americans. They will soon be here, just wait – in buses wrapped in cellophane, and with dosimeters, always with dosimeters, bringing with them their own food and water. We'll end up saying: Welcome to Chernobyl tourism. Maybe the worst of the destructions is that dignity has been thrown to the ground. Self-respect for a Belorussian is more important than love, than water, than food. Just the same, it will not take a long time. Look at the Incas. They died out in the course of four seasons. God, we are dying, God. The life of the living is death. And here sits a hoarse devil, chattering, and has not noticed that his mouth has become an arsehole. No, mate, distance needn't lose courage.

Dmitri's throat rumbles like he should have been a turkey. He gobbles all the time, and people suppose he is angry or dangerous. Dmitri becomes dangerous because people believe he is dangerous. He goes out in the evenings along the zone, scouting. The zone is the boundary. Dmitri walks along every evening, wondering what would happen if he crossed over the boundary. Would he notice the radiation there? Would the guards come running? Are there other people inside the zone? Dmitri thinks of nothing but the zone, roams around the barriers, roams for long stretches. One evening he sees a button just inside the barrier. He must have that button. He makes up his mind to cross the invisible visible boundary and go inside. He takes a knife and a torch with him and goes inside, into the darkness. He walks without being seen, can't see himself, simply walks. Far away are the chimneys of the power plant. He goes towards some abandoned houses. It is perfectly quiet, but for the rumbling in his throat. He has the button in his pocket. The button shines. Can he feel the radiation? The houses are empty, but the furniture is still there. Outside, there are untended flowerbeds nobody has touched for years. He walks through all the houses. From one of them, he hears the sound of somebody standing absolutely still. He listens, the other listens. He then throws away the button, which rolls over the floor and makes more noise than his rumbling. I'm not rumbling, thinks Dmitri. A hand stretches out and picks up the button. It becomes quiet again. Dmitri thinks he can hear the light of his torch. He can't stand it any more and shouts 'hello'.

It is four o'clock in the morning, the toughest hour in the night watch. Sergei struggles to keep awake. He hasn't had any sleep in the day either, the youngest son kept crying the whole time. He sits gazing at the control panel, everything is in order in D Area. His head falls on his chest. In his dream, he wakes up at the youngest son's bawling. Behind him is the control panel, flashing all over, run wild. All is normal, but he saw something.

Jura comes in and asks for the red ball. I don't know if he has a red ball, but help him look for it; it is the quickest way to get to sit down on the sofa again. We find it in the cupboard out in the passage, with the other beach things. He runs out again and I sit down. Stretching out my legs, I rest my brain against my skull. The red warning lights on the instrument desk blink. I see them but suddenly can't remember what I'm supposed to do. My foot kicks at a red ball, it doesn't stop blinking. I kick and kick, and the ball grows bigger. Then there are more balls, sirens, but no noise. Jura stands looking at me. I realize he has been standing there for a while. He has the ball in his arms. Someone is shouting – comes into the control room and shouts I don't understand what. Jura drops the ball and runs out. I scream. The alarm lights change colour all the time. I can't get out. Don't know how Jura found the door, the control room is so small. I press the ball into the middle of the floor wanting to make a hole, but I can't manage it.

Alyoshya plays fireman, empties sand. He is going to do what Father did. He empties sand until the fire goes out and builds a sarcophagus around the reactor. Svetlana sighs, the child is unruly and bothers her. And she has to manage everything alone, never gets to go out by herself. Alyoshya cries out, making car sounds. Svetlana holds on, holds onto the fact that her son is not ill. But her husband, he was one of the first ones to die. She couldn't even reach the hospital in time. He! Her husband! The taste of him, his blood, semen. All the crazy madness, the smell of his socks, the small, light traces of excrement, drifting round in the toilet after he had flushed. Well, it was we who were going to be the happiest ones. There is no meaning now. The days are without hours. She forgets the child and thinks that hatred is yellow, a yellow cloud inside her head that contaminates everything. The boy does not forget. Not her nor him. She is not allowed to dream herself back. She should have been cooking dinner now. She vomits yellow orange juice over Alyoshya's drawing book – yellow vomit, a yellow cloud. She goes to the woman in the neighbouring house and borrows vodka… There's warmth in your hands. It's lovely to swing on your arm, swing madly in a tango step. You are here, we are dancing. I swing, you swing me – how strong you have become… Wait, I am just going to take another swig. Do you see my high heels? They are for you. How young we are! You smell cool, even though the dance is hot. I am hot too. I think I must sit down for a bit. Sit beside me, dream me a dream to dance in. I talk too much, I will be absolutely quiet now. Listen how quiet I am. No, I'm laughing, laughing and laughing – funny you!

Vladim, dance is… oh, you?

Tired, I am

So tired, my love. Sleep

Tomorrow be

here

Svetlana resists. She does not want to wake up. She knows what she is going to wake up to.

Tomorrow is the memorial ceremony, it is fifteen years since the funeral. Fifteen years since the wedding. Svetlana goes about making preparations. She feels nothing. She moves the crystal flower vase. Would she feel anything if she smashed the vase and cut herself on the broken glass? She is waiting to see Vladim come in at the door soon. It is ten past ten and the evening shift is over. Maybe he is dropping into the bar for a drink before he comes home. That's fine, so long as you get up again in the morning.

Remember, you have promised Alyoshya to help him repair his bicycle...? Alyoshya stands in the doorway: Mummy, he won't come this evening either, you know that. The fourteen-year-old has something hard in his face. Dead, Mummy, dead, dead, dead!

If a windmill overturns, will it cause changes in the genetic material of an embryo?

Biological Half-life

Biological half-life is a measurement for how fast a substance is expelled through the excretory system. How quickly radioactive substances get expelled from the body depends on which part of the body the substances are absorbed into. Cesium binds to blood and musculature and will be expelled more rapidly than Strontium, which binds to the skeleton. The biological half-life therefore varies from substance to substance, from species to species, and with the age and development of the individual.

I am reading about Marie Curie. I have to write an exercise about her, who worked with radiation all her life and died of leukaemia; she never took care and let herself be irradiated by whatever she was working with. While the other students are in the canteen, I shall feed myself with books. I will pick out what is important. I will make an important discovery. I look at the picture of Madame Curie on the back of the book: What did you think, Marie, when you discovered, for the first time, that new substance that nobody had seen in its pure form before? It is discipline, it is discipline it pivots on, to hold itself steady if it wobbles. Ideal conditions do not exist. One has to just work and keep control on oneself. It's all about what one chooses to do when one should have done something else. The courage to be what one believes in, the courage for alternatives, to break away from the ordinary. I will become alone, a cripple without crutches, I will manage it. I will discover something that helps the radiation-injured, something to relieve the pain. Maybe I can be like the girl in the fairytale, the little girl in a strange forest, with a forest floor that wants to suck her feet down the hill. The girl tries to walk, she walks and walks all alone. She does not recognize anything. Everything is different. When she has walked for many hours, an arm suddenly appears out of nowhere. A hand without a body, it reaches out to her. She takes it and lets herself be led to the edge of the forest. She knows where she is and has only to take the path home, but when she turns round she sees the hand beckoning, and she decides to follow it into the forest again. That is where she is supposed to be. In the forest, she becomes a hand that helps other people, those who have gone astray, to find their way out or into the forest forever.

I chew on my hair and think I will read about the great atomic scientists and stay in their forest. By the way, do atoms have a taste, a smell? Madame Curie was killed by her own research, imagine that. I see for myself that the hands, which embraced her daughters, had brown spots. She worked so hard, I admire her. I really wonder what she felt when she first saw the new substance, the element she isolated – the one that radiates. Did she know it was dangerous? That what she was involved in could do great damage? The Nobel Prize... I wonder what she said to Pierre, did she say it quite matter-of-factly? We got the Nobel Prize today. We got the lease on the house today. I would so much like to know. I don't know what I would have thought. I could never have done that; I am too scared. It must have been cold in that little bedsit of hers; I can almost feel you shivering, Marie. I can't do that, I only think it. I shiver too. They look happy in photos, cycling in the parks of Paris, and out in the countryside; they cycled a lot. Madame Curie, help me. I want to be a strong and important woman. I want to do something new, something nobody believes I can achieve. Did she get a laurel wreath or only a medal? The laurel wreath was certainly big enough for two, one that could be used in cooking. Were her little girls allowed to try it on? Were they afraid of her? I must go out and buy bread. The queue is always long before I join it. You also forgot such things, you too, Marie, I am sure of it. It's not so far to walk. I don't need a bicycle, but I cycle and then I go into a café. I believe there are more substances to discover, things that are important, not dangerous; they don't have to be dangerous to be important. Isn't that so? My hands don't have brown spots. They are newly washed, white. I look at the other people. A man smokes right down to the filter. It looks as if his wife has a breast missing. I watch them. They don't seem to notice me. They talk quietly together. I was given good advice once: Keep yourself busy. In the evenings too. Someone has altered the hammer and sickle picture to a hammer and a banana, yellow and red and funny. Self-esteem is the most important thing, more important than the esteem of others; they don't depend on each other in any case. Quite definitely not. There I had an idea of my own. A complete one. Independent of Curie or the accident. Maybe I am able to think, I'll think about that. I'll meet a man who is smaller than myself. How do I know that? It might be quite the opposite, or I am steering myself towards what I believe. I know I am thinking. I am thinking about thinking – how I should have thought. More importantly, how I should have thought bigger. Then I'll look for a position. A job in an office, take an apple with me, eat it in the break while I chat with my colleagues. Colleagues, that will be good. We'll chat about other things as well. Have a drink together now and then. I have a sore on my cheek. It's a sore, not a pimple. I don't know which is worse, to know or not to know. Am I ill? I don't have the heaviness of women, women who are heavy in their bodies, who know where it is. I imagine a development, that it will all go upwards, that my stomach will be more prominent under the sweater. I was born just after the accident, I can't help thinking however much I try. I don't think about it, not every day in any case. Curie turns away and goes, I see only the white top of her hair. And I remember her hands.

People are so sour... They could have smiled at least.... Is that so dangerous? I'll try doing it, smile so that people take notice. Look at me when I walk around, without crying. I won't cry. I'll finish kissing them and go on laughing. The café door is hard to close. It's getting cold, I feel the draught around my legs. It is Friday already, and the chemistry test is on Monday. That's the one I'll do best in, I just know that. The sore on my cheek is a sign that the cancer is going to come. I begin every day by checking it. No sign on the skin, only in the mind. I imagine a force that rises up, all brightness, warmth and love. I call upon it. Myths. There are not many shamans left in Siberia now, they have crossed the border to death. They did not manage to turn back to the body that lay waiting. I have heard French songs. Did you hear them too, Curie, now and then, after a spell of work at the laboratory? Or were you strict with yourself? I was always strict with my dolls. My mother asked how I had learnt to shake and scold them. I think this is a good sign. This seat is taken. Just move, it will not come true. Don't you hear? I am strict. I like it. I am strictest with myself, but not always when I am thinking. The thoughts are not strict enough. They just come and go, without my deciding anything much. I am angry before I have finished thinking them, not happy. For that, I must have to think for quite a long time. Is this normal or do I have a tendency to be melancholy? I have some old posters stuck on the window, and I don't get any air. It is not good for the thoughts, for they think more narrowly, far too narrowly. Inside a bag, arms that stretch out, feet that struggle. In the bag, a white bag, like an egg, the membrane around a foetus, a balloon. A balloon is best, for balloons burst the easiest. They can rise up, ballooning journeys, over the Poles, fall down into a crevasse… Green is the last thing you see… Oh, I think myself away. I must be stricter… The sound has gone away from my shouts, can you hear? Is anyone listening? Curie, don't go… Don't do it for real. I am quite, quite alone, aren't I? Just laugh. I could have laughed myself, but I am inside the bag, and it is only getting whiter; there's white against my eye. Weird, weird, weird, that's what I am, I know it. Hold on, I don't think that, I know. That is why the teacher likes me. If he didn't like me, I would not have got such good marks.

I have hung up a poster above my desk that says: 'Read a lot for the exam!' The exam is next year, but I have already started preparing. That's the ticket. Exactly like Madame Curie. She had to earn money for her brothers and sisters before she could go to Paris and study. She was a governess for several years. That I will never be. Not to nouveau riche Armenian nor lazy Russian kids. They can do as I do, learn English by themselves. All you have to do is read and speak aloud in your own room. Think, thought, or was it thaugth. I have found my dictionary and open it at random at words with 'psy': psychosomatic, for example. It is only to feed the brain.

Now an hour has gone by. The Chernobyl monument looks like a brain with a hole. There is air or sky in the hole. In front of it stands a person who is not well. Actually the monument is supposed to represent a radioactive cloud, an atomic mushroom, but I think it's the brain that's the problem. I wonder whether I would have been different if I hadn't had the same name as Marie Curie. A bit more relaxed, maybe. Then I would not have cried because I have a whole book to read before Monday. 284 pages. I'll never get through it.

I don't think I'd like to die for an invention, but Curie could surely not have known how dangerous her research was. And afterwards, it was too late. When the spots appeared on her hands, she could do nothing but carry on. What if she had known before she began: 'You will get two Nobel Prizes in exchange for an early death?' All the firemen who sacrificed themselves during the accident, did they know, or didn't they, what would happen to them? Would I have gone in if I had known, I don't think so. Am I a Marie, am I leftovers, left over from the others, those who survived. Can I stop thinking, is it possible to halt it just for a second, like when the heart misses a beat? A pocket. How does it feel there? Can one rest in it? Or is that what death is, that silence? At school they have received a personal computer, the noises from the keyboard are deafening. The students should have had vitamins, they fall asleep. The girls suffer, they become fat when their metabolisms fail. Many are disorganized. Some of the children were able to travel to the West in summer, to Ireland, Norway, Switzerland, Austria. They come back with red cheeks and other dreams. Nothing here counts any more. They must go there, must have everything. It is not right. They will become unfree people, slaves to things and shallow entertainment. Must I admonish like that? I am young. I must not think about it. I want to have a different mind, with straighter lines, not warped. Maybe I can become the president, the first woman president, Catherine the Great. I could have succeeded in that. I have the ideas and can rise up where I want to. There are many signs. The light in the corridor is dim, no intellectual ladies come to this café. A pity because I have taught myself their words. They say women's struggle, sexual liberation, oppression, Mill, free abortion. The philosophers say identity, aesthetics, ethics, consciousness, perception. And the politicians say budget, analysis, international, strategic, corruption, dismissal. They do not say pollution. The words of others overlay mine and mix in my mouth. You don't need a key, it is wide open – just help yourself.

Hops grow by the wall of the house, and the calves lie chewing the cud. People live in the wood store, those who moved from the zone and had no relatives. The wood weeps and is wet when the woman puts it in the oven. Outside, are the old grave stones. We shift them, one by one, but never find anything. An elderly man goes by, pushing a pram. A puppy lies in the pram, it blinks and looks contented. Sawdust in the eyes, mari, mari, marigold. We look out into the rain. We were all out in the rain. Saw the clouds coming with the radioactivity, the rain was just as shiny. We showered the spring in ourselves. The illness trickled into our ears, rainwater went down the throat and up our noses. We let the roots of our hair be soaked, they were thirsty too. The days were coloured like flax, like corn and something that was old in us… 'This spring is our spring'… Maybe we still believe it, and keep washing it out in another water.

There are small rodents under the corn. She stepped on one. It moved under her foot and became still before she had time to move. Now she is careful where she walks. She is going into the town to meet friends. They will notice that she has lost all her hair... If only she had been able to keep it until her birthday; she will be seventeen on Thursday. But so much fell out when she showered... and every morning the pillow was covered. She just had to cut off the little that was left on top. They will not say anything, nobody says anything about such things. Everyone knows, there are so many who have lost their hair now. She saw herself in the mirror and hid it. She has taken down the mirror in the living room as well. She looks like a bun, a very old man. She won't get to meet any man. Men want women with long curls, or a short smooth fashionable hairstyle, or shoulder-length hair. Not one as hairless as a day-old baby mouse, pale pink and repulsive. She is going to meet her friends. It is better they see her first. She will need them at school to dare to go up the steps. She cries until the puddle is full. It is good that it is raining. Why did I have to lose my hair? Couldn't I have had something that doesn't show? She reaches the door of the youth centre. The others are sitting and chatting. She waits, knowing that they will become absolutely silent when they see her. She runs out again, doesn't see what she is stepping on. She should have dared to steal from a shop. She could have bought a wig. I want to be me. She rubs her skull with pepper vodka. Father, light it!

You walk along a street in Minsk, in the part of town where the Chernobyl people live. The washed clothes on the little glass balconies are as colourless as the blocks of flats. You could have lived there, but you are only on a visit. You have a cake with you, what else could you do. You got away, something or the other grew in you, awakened, wanted to go forward – it refused to disappear in the accident. The old women with headscarves sit on benches outside the flats. They have brought along their habits with them from the villages they moved from. They sit without really talking. They all know each other's stories; they need strangers. You take a little detour out in the road. You cannot bear the conversation about the dead children, the drunk husbands, and pensions that don't arrive, nor bear to hear how beautiful it was in their village at this time of the year.

⁓

It is drizzling. She is on the way down to the old town. She feels that she does not belong here. Her feet are not used to the cobblestones on the way to the Chernobyl Museum. She's going there to look at the sign for the village she comes from. There is a sign for each village that was destroyed. They hang from the ceiling in the entrance hall to the museum, seventy signs in all. She usually goes to the museum a couple of times a year to say hello. For her, the accident became an opportunity for a completely different life, a life she could not have seen for herself before the accident. Before that, there was only the village, school, their spot of land and the collective far away, where both her parents worked. She was moved away, first to a summer camp for four months instead of two. There was no one to talk to. She didn't dare to make friends with anyone, they would soon have to part after all. That long plait of hers, which they cut off the first day, she wasn't allowed to hold it in her hands afterwards. It was to be burnt, they said. And she remembered the smell of singed hair from the time she bent over the candles during mass, when her fringe and eyelashes had been burnt away. High heels on cobblestones, it's difficult. She must be aware of each step. She regrets wanting to look elegant. She sees the signs. One of them belongs to the neighbouring village her grandfather came from. He said 'raspberry' differently from Grandmother, Mummy and herself. She does not stop at the signs as she usually does, just goes on up the stairs and into the first room with the firemen and the clock that has stopped at 01.23.

There was a man at the station that morning who fell and was trampled. Mummy and I did not arrive until later. Under my vest, next to my chest, Mummy had fastened a bit of paper with my name on it, and Uncle's name and address. That was where I was going. Then onwards to the summer camp by the Volga. The paper tickled. On the bus to Kiev, I had to stand the whole way. It is difficult to hold your balance when you want to hide your eyes.

At first in Kiev, Mummy kept chickens on the veranda. One day one of them grew up into a cock and crowed loudly at four o'clock in the morning. Mummy did not want to be seen, so she did not dare go out and fetch it in. People were so angry with the cock, and we missed them all terribly. But now it is so long ago, everyone wants to forget. And I am the only one from where we live who goes to the museum. Our blocks of flats are like a contemporary museum, with living people, living illnesses, outcries from behind padded doors in the evenings. Some have got up, but they don't want to speak to those who cry.

The sun comes out and I can see my shadow on the wall. Unthinkingly I go out and stand by the old market. My hair is short, I wonder if I would have given a different impression with plaits down to my waist and a shawl over my head. Back in the village, I would have been a married woman by now.

The first time she learnt something about language was through a little sign in the aisle of the bus going away from the zone. Something was written in foreign letters, which the teacher said was written in the Latin alphabet. It must have been Swedish. It said something about buggies being put here in the aisle. She remembers that she stared at the sign the whole journey, made up her mind to understand the letters that said 'buggies can be put here' one day.

I am not allowed to play with the others. The other children are afraid of me. They say I radiate, and that we should not be here. Go home, that's what Mummy and Papa say too. My shoes bore down into the sand in the playground outside the entrance. Soon they will not look new any longer. But they bore down just the same, making the pit bigger and bigger. Have they cut your hair off? asks a girl with long brown hair. The others laugh. It was sure to be so full of radiation that it set itself alight. They laugh again. I have hidden my plait, it lies in a plastic bag far inside in the new cupboard. Mother knows it is there, but she has not said anything. Hope you won't be in our class, shout the girls. How old are you anyway? They shout again. But I don't reply. Imagine if I have to go into their class! I dare not. They will tell everyone that I am from the zone, that I am dangerous. They must never see my sister, she is retarded... And that may be because Father helped with the clearing up, but it is not certain, says Father – that sort of thing can happen regardless.

Fedora had to move to a different place from us. We sat in the garden and talked about it, that we should say a proper goodbye to each other and exchange addresses and we should never forget each other, and go and visit when we were bigger. Suddenly one day, they had simply gone, before I could get their new address. We had time for nothing... Something must have happened. Perhaps her mother died... I will put an ad in the newspaper and search for her. There are people on the radio all the time, asking about their relatives. The announcer says, person so-and-so is looking for person so-and-so. I will make contact through the office. She has not forgotten me, I know that... Maybe the girls where she moved to are horrible too...?

My husband planted a tree for each child we had. I remember he had gone out and fetched a fine birch sapling with a thin, stark white trunk. He made me step outside, even though I was so exhausted after the birth. It felt like we were doing something important.

Our boy died just before he turned eight. His birch tree withered the same winter. In the spring, it was quite dry, and when my husband dug it up, I saw him crying. Now we dare not look at the other three birch trees planted around the house.

I often wonder what happened to my baby rabbit. Before we left, while the buses stood waiting and the soldiers bellowed, I ran to open the hutch and it hopped out. Maybe it knew that all the cats and big dogs had also been let loose and that there were foxes in the woods behind the flats. I had promised Father not to cry. On the bus, I just stared out of the window, looking for wild rabbits. Later I taught myself to cry inside, for tears can just as easily fall on the inside as on the outside where they show. All you have to do is bend your head a bit backwards, just a bit. You don't even have to close your eyelids. Just let it drip downwards on the other side of the skin, over the warm meat and the white flesh. On the cheekbones and right down into the stomach; actually there is a little container there that collects tear water. Tear water is bluer than ordinary water, both transparent and blue, like the Northern Lights. Imagine being out in space when the Northern Lights appear! Maybe I can be a vet, then I can help animals who have got sick. But the vet has to put down the old animals, or the injured… After the accident there were many, many animals which had to be put down. I could never have borne to do that.

The plane comes lower than I have ever seen before. It flies between the treetops. I can see the pilot clearly, he has no eyes, only a helmet. Far out on a branch lies a bird's nest. The noise of the plane sends a terror through the nest. The baby birds cower back. One backs itself right out and smashes against the hill while the plane roars past.

A woman wanted to send her children away but could not afford to. She wrote letters to the authorities, without getting any reply. She said they know more than we think they keep quiet about. There is whispering on the stairs about others who know. There is so much whispering on the stairs that the whispers linger as a hum, a sigh... And now and then, a scream... We call it the scream on the stairs. It is uncanny to hear it when one is quite alone. I dare not whisper there, I rush down the steps and out into the street. The wind is blowing. Leaves and a letter blow up in the air. A letter, which is on the way to its address but just has to take a little flight first, a great effort without direction. I must get away from here, I can't breathe in the wind. I am Galina, and I can't breathe, can't whisper, and my scream lives on the stairs. You have to experience me a little slowly. We are floating. It is as slow as wool. It could have gone in another direction, like coal. The leaves fall differently from us. I am in something I can't see... No, I'm not thinking properly, that's not the way it works. Something has begun eating you and does not want to stop. The wormwood star fell. It was in the daytime and nobody noticed it. The day nobody saw is unnatural. We could have spoken about that here, but there is cottonwool in our mouths, cottonwool around our thoughts – they are not able to emerge as thoughts. I can't remember how I think, how things relate to each other and become something I have understood. I had a cart, I always thought of Mother Courage, the children should have been acted by old people, the cart filled with what I couldn't remember, small pieces of learning about what I had done. Later I will cry, now I simply can't manage to cry. Crying is afraid, afraid of what it craves.

We were the gang from Poltava district. We met every Saturday evening, only us Afghanistan veterans, always on the plain, near Dneper, but never on the peninsula itself, that bright, sand-sculpted landmark out in the water. It is best there, but too many people. Everyone wanted to sit together, even after the sun went down with the warmth. We made a bonfire, roasted chickens, drank warm wine and played the bandura. I was usually the one who picked it up. After the accident, gatherings like that became impossible. Taras was already dead, and Galina had become quiet, she hung on for three days... Little Mikhail, the angel... well, he was saved, or what should we say. No songs are sad enough. The bandura must be untuned and smashed against the stones we sat on. Mikhail, forgive me. It will soon be dark again, I'll get the bandura out again. Mikhail, I can hear your wings. You are laughing, aren't you?

Chisel strikes steadily. There's a rhythm that is interrupted now and then. He listens for the next blow... Hard to stop when you have started... There it comes, good... Wait for the next, wait. Hey, come back, we have to get more sandbags. The boss shouts, he does not like what he sees. A boy should not be staring up at the sky when he has a helmet on his head. He should look for something to do, keep going. They get inside the little truck. It is yellow and the boy thinks the front looks like a face, two shining eyes and a mouth. The boss reverses; it is good to sit down. They drive impatiently towards the town, hearing the gravel against the wheels.

It is cramped in the small cabin. It smells of building site, mortar, earth, dirty shoes, the man and the boy. Half a year has gone by since the accident. It no longer smells of fire. It is no longer dangerous, said the boss the first day, but only old women believe that. Now Reactor Three has to be enclosed.We'll make that safe, said the boss. It is quiet inside the truck. The boy tries to think of something to talk about, something important, so that the boss will realize that he understands things, knows things, that he is aware… What should he say? He can't think of anything. He is not used to talking to grown-up men. There have only been Mummy and friends. No men who are big and serious like the boss. Does he enjoy the job? Is he afraid? Does he think about the accident at all? I won't ask about that. Now I must say something. Why doesn't he say anything? He could have cracked a joke, asked about school, or the family.

The boss pays attention to the boy, menacingly. So long as he does not ask, and it is best not to ask. That way we can survive everything, not let anything touch us – go to work, don't think that it is dangerous, just get on with things, calmly and simply. The boy looks out of the window and at the boss at the same time, his coarse face reflecting in the windowpane. What was he like when he was young? What were his cheeks like then? The boss sees that he sees and looks away at the road. There are no cars, it is completely flat. And it is so cramped inside the truck, their jackets rub against each other and are heard clearly when everything is so quiet. Oh, say something then, why can't he just say something? Ask if I am enjoying myself, if I want to go on working here… Is he in a bad mood? He's tired out maybe.

The boy is going to ask whether I am enjoying it, if it is a good job. What am I going to answer? I don't know, I don't want to think about it. He is not like me, he is much too weak. It is too quiet here, we should have had a radio. They don't make that a priority, oh no. What is he thinking about? I can see he is thinking. Just say it. It is better than this silence. I can get back at him, tell him he mustn't worry, that there's no sense in asking. What do I have to say to him? What would I have asked about twenty years ago, what did I know then? It is a long time ago... What has happened in these years? I have gone to work, come home – was it good, am I doing all right?

What is he thinking about? thinks the boy, just as quiet. I have nobody else to ask, nobody else who knows. What is it like to live like this? Is it good? Will I do all right? He smells of tobacco. I can ask for some tobacco perhaps.

The fly's proboscis explores my skin. Surely it has not had sugar, thinks Oleg. It is a pity that a fly should never get to taste sugar. Oleg has hidden away a little from before the accident, kept it hidden: Maybe I will need it one day, one never knows... When he fetches a bit to give to the fly, he sees that the sugar has gone blue. Even though I packed it in both paper and plastic, says Oleg out loud. The children are playing outside, they have never had sugar either. Then it is quiet. Oleg is expecting his pension. It may come today or tomorrow. He thinks it will come today. I can tell it by the flies. They are biting. They know that today they will get to see food on the table. They look forward to buzzing round my food, that is why they are so happy now. Oleg thinks about his sugar: I should have done as the birds do. They hide their seeds in the bark of trees. Oleg is drunk. The pension lies at the side of the ditch and the flies are hungry. Oleg dreams of sugar, white and blue sugar poured over each other. The leaves of the mulberry tree against a dark sky is the first thing he sees when he wakes up and feels ashamed of himself, feels small and old.

The telephone began to ring. It hardly ever rang before, but now it rings several times a day. It's always the same, nobody answers or says hello; just a void at the end of the wire. Father has stopped picking it up, Mother does it when she can't bear the ringing any longer. Grandfather thinks it is something wrong, something we have done, that it is the police, the surveillance, or someone who wants to destroy us. The telephone is hidden in the closet, we hear it just the same. Grandfather says it has changed colour. That it was red before, and now it is brown, or I don't know – I haven't had a look at it for a long time. It never leaves us in peace. We go out of the house, but when we come back in there's the ringing again in the wall, like an echo – the telephone has spoken. Gradually the telephone began to talk. It asked us to listen carefully, an important message was going to come soon. What was strange was that we all heard the same thing, it could not be only imagination. Grandfather doesn't imagine anything whatsoever. The telephone spoke in riddles, none of us understood it. Now and then it mentioned a name, I am certain of that. At last we got tired of the telephone talking, so we took out the plug and put the device in the cellar. And I wonder whether I can hear noises from there at night, a voice talking and talking – what would happen if I lifted the receiver and answered?

Why did Father suddenly decide to treat us to a trip just that weekend? The long trip in the riverboat down the Dneper from Kiev and all the way to the Black Sea and Odessa. Mother played movie star and sat looking beautiful, read novels and smoked cigarettes, I had a new sun hat so as not to get too many freckles, and my little brother ran up and down and became friends with the engineer. Father had worked double shifts at the plant the last week to be able to afford to go. Now he dozed in the deckchair, batted away an insect now and then, looked proudly up at Mother as if he wanted to shout that he was some husband and father and a senior engineer who had done well for himself. I was shy and happy, peeped at a boy who was also on board; he was very goodlooking. Now we are married. When we reached Odessa, Father got a telegram. He had to travel back at once but ordered us to stay on the boat. He gave Mother all the money he had and climbed into a waiting Volga. We did not know much, but we knew that the fantasy changed its course and went haywire. Are all the people we know dead? Grandmother, has anyone contacted her? Mother ran about, shouted that we were not to drink milk. I stood in the passage outside our cabin and talked with Anton for the first time. His big sister was a cleaner at the plant, and he forgot to act tough; he was only terrified. We walked about on the deck that evening and talked about our friends, all the schoolmates who were to be at the First of May event in Kiev. Mother called us in. She had got hold of iodine tablets. I shared mine with Anton. Sometimes we think if it had not been for the accident, we might never have met each other.

Everyone in Father's department had protective clothing on during the clean-up, but he forgot himself. Our son, Jaroslav, is named after him. Father died ten days before Jaroslav 'came into the world' – that is such a lovely expression – and the sorrow over Father blended into the joy about the growing child. We lived with relatives of Anton's then, outside Moscow. Even though Father was weak at that time, he never gave up, and so we had to move before the birth. It could still be too late, I heard him say to Mother once. But Jaroslav is healthy and strong and has already decided to be an engineer when he grows up, just like Grandfather. But not at the plant, I say then, and he looks at me with big, much too mature eyes, and answers: No way, I'm going to build bridges, high bridges that riverboats can drive underneath. He has already been on the riverboats several times. We go to Kiev once a year, always towards the end of April, and take Mother with us down the slow way, while we think of Father.

The cardboard boxes are white, like coffins. The car is a larger coffin, loaded with many boxes full of our lives, sofa cushions, albums. Things we would have saved from a fire are moved. The neighbours stand around, making small talk and feeling envious, thinking they should also have had somewhere to go, friends or relatives. The car sets off. Don't turn around now. Wait until it is no longer dangerous. When does it stop being dangerous? There's a throbbing in the head, as if you are about to catch a cold, all the time. The car is badly packed in a hurry. It is too late anyway. The throbbing accompanies us. Always to be from there, even when you are asleep. The car drives in the dark with the load, people and things that belong together, things that will become something else in a new place, a different sound in the clock on the wall. Great-grandmother's needle-work curls up, it is affected by the journey; it had always hung in the same place. Don't think such things. Just jump out of the car. Carry the boxes even if you don't have the energy, or haven't had the energy for a long time. Carry anyway so that the car can return empty... It would be easier to drive it maybe... you won't find out. The beds are not ready. They must be put up. The mattress has spots of damp. It rained and the tarpaulin had a hole we couldn't see by torchlight. We put up the beds, get the quilts out of the plastic. Nobody speaks. Lie down without a hug. In order to last out. You are good at that. The skin has large holes. Not to know where the light switch is when you have to go to the loo... You must have fallen asleep anyway. Even if you thought you lay awake, lay awake without thinking, only wept – wept dark and wept light, no thoughts coming through.

Like a coating, new days fall, layer upon layer. Feet get used to the roads... There are the four first times you don't know where to go. And then you go without thinking. It is almost easy. Just about open the eyelids, a film hangs there, dimming the sight, refracts the light too early and it becomes grey. No point in sending letters. Best like this, that is what everyone thinks. The car has returned now, just as white and square, with new coffins. Some cases are left behind, no car will come and fetch them anyway. The cactus suddenly flowers, it never did that there. There is going to be a theme exhibition here. About the accident. You are asked to help, to talk about it. Nobody can bear to. The exhibition is open for several weeks at the library. You can sneak in and look. There are pictures in there. There is something that looks like me – a face, with a spot, maybe a mole, a birthmark, maybe a Chernobyl spot. A spot like the others. Why look at it again. Nobody asks. They think they know they will be writing about the accident in textbooks, the teachers will be talking about it while they are thinking about lunch, while the students scribble their names in roughbooks, or pick something from under a nail. It will soon come to this.

We are history. Whatever happened here will be talked and written about for a long time. We are included in history, it concerns us, not wretched people in a faraway country, like in the news broadcasts. Earthquakes, people freezing outside emergency tents, starry nights and misery. The light from a TV camera goes out quickly, does not give warmth. Floods in Bangladesh, swamped rice paddies, famine. This time it is us, but we are alive – we want so much to live. Shall we believe in radiation we can't see? Everything is different. It is not worth dreaming any more. It is a pity for us, and there is no help. Many people just want to go on as before. Maybe that is best. We do not know anything else. The TV cameras have all gone. New catastrophes are striking other places. But we are left to stay on after the transmission.

We could not even see the power plant from our village, only the light, dimmed by distance, a milky white haze. How were we to know it could be so dangerous? And what could we have done even if we had known? We *could have* moved away or relied on everything going well, for it was important for the economy, for the Soviet – it was necessary for all of us... could we? We can't see into the future. But why we chose not to ask... And now, I am so tired, so tired all the time that I can't ask any more. I know it is the first stage of radiation sickness. The accident will break the Soviet Union into pieces, I am sure of it. Think how people felt, those who lived through the German invasion, Gulag, the revolution. Think how they were involved in historic events, how the world looked on and wanted to see it from outside, without being able to understand it in the least.

Soon I won't have the energy to think at all, but there are other people who will think, who will demand answers and bring the guilty to account. I don't have the energy to see it through.

Days go by. There's no reason to keep a diary. A diary is for a life in which something happens. I wait, not expecting anything to happen. I could have moved, I could have spoken up. I wash her trousers and sweaters. I let the cat out and make something that resembles tea, but unaware that I am doing it. I don't look back. No letters arrive. There's nothing to say. I don't have to write this. There is no difference, thoughts won't develop. Mother is old, I can't abandon her. I will become like her, have only some more years to wait. I never became a teacher. I could have been one. Then I would have had my own flat. I think I have to laugh. It is sunny, I could have gone for a walk. There are the white anemones from when I was small, they hang in the trees and don't reflect the light. Someone has dried them, without thinking how sad they look. The white leaves drift down, looking like spring snow. I trample on the snow, it is just as soft but dry. The rubbish dumps are also covered in snow, but the bicycle wheels and old fridges are not hidden. Someone has thrown away a fridge, it must have been a long time ago. I want white anemones, not a fridge. I am still waiting, the diary page is nearly filled up. I begin to stop. So slowly it goes, stopping, the writing. It takes ten minutes to get coal from the cellar. The water has gone, the pipes gurgle, maybe one is bursting; it can take half a day. Aurora cigarettes don't taste like Stars. They used to. To wait just a bit… It doesn't help to make tea. Who is going to be longing for my tea? The cat can be set free. I'll set Mother free – she will go to where there is light. It is not far. Just that one dark street, and then there is light enough to see. I continue to write. I write everything down. Three cigarettes left before the decision. I feel the ring on my right hand. It is Father's wedding ring. Altered to my size when he died. I know it so well, it is easy to take it off; the knuckles don't protest, they yield. I hang the ring up beside the mirror; it doesn't shine, it is much too dull, too worn. I could fill my overcoat with stones; that might work. It will clatter nicely in the river. The coal has burnt out and it is cold, but I don't seem to freeze. Someone might phone, then I must say that it isn't convenient. That would be fine. One cigarette left. I don't light it. That will be a surprise. I am going out to walk. There's a direction. It is not about me finding it, it will find me when the time is right. It has been quiet for a long time, longer than usual... Is Mother sleeping? I don't look back. I don't look back at anything. It is dark enough. It should be dark; the soft mark on my face is hidden in the dark. Nobody can see what I look like.

The cigarette is long, its glow is an eye. I take off my sweater, the shirt falls off by itself. It is difficult to smoke at the same time, so I put the cigarette down. That way it will last a little longer. I know what I don't want, it can get much worse. Eyedrops in the throat, they taste salty. I'll write until I go. I'm going soon, out in the direction of the water. Nothing will be ugly – it is milk mixed with tea, a bit dirtier but rounder. This is something I read somewhere: 'I take you on my back and carry you forward.' I'm going. It is like before. I know something is decided, I'll simply go along with it. Just as I hope, I'm going, I will go. I get up, will get up. There is the door, the overcoat hangs on the back of it. There is the door... the overcoat with the stones... Mother calls out.

The cement floor has a damp patch. That is all that is left of my dog. I hold it wrapped in a rug. Its nose is dry and soft brown eyes are turned upwards. I will bury it soon. Just wait a little, for it's still warm, it is still nearly warm. If I ripped it open, it would be full of tumours. The bumps can be felt under the fur. There have been so many burials... maybe this one will be the hardest. I will never get myself another dog, not as long as we live here. Nobody can warn animals against becquerel. It always knew that it was fond of me, imagine. I had only to come in and it went quite wild with joy. Now and then it bit me round the wrist and held me fast when I had been too long at the hospital. I let myself be bitten.

It is dark and cold at the library. They have to save electricity. Soon we won't even be able to borrow books any more. But the brown chairs are good. I bring a small torch with me and read with my gloves on. At home, I am not allowed to read books like these. Books with poetry. The little poems with the nervous line divisions. I press the books against my chest, press hard and feel something tighten within. Father wants me to read 'proper literature' as he calls it, political theory and philosophy. It must be about will, the will to change, he says. I should read about atomic accidents, radioactivity, the risk of radiation... But after the accident, all such books were removed from the library. One of the lecturers at the university is sure to have some, but I don't want to read them. I want to sit here in the dark, and read and sniff the aroma of French restaurants, spices, or listen to the swoop of a swallow catching an insect, maybe a little brown fly. While Rousseau turns away in his forest, I can turn away from the smell of coal and cabbage... I want to read about snow. Snow that lays itself quietly and rests on the ice, under which the swallows have hidden themselves at the bottom of a lake. I have dandruff on my fingers. It has sprinkled a white dust on my sweater. It drifts down towards the book. Particles of me are left there.

'Through all the years, centuries, millenia that have gone by before I was born and the millenia that will go by after I am dead, stretch two identical oceans of darkness, with my life, a shining spark, in between. It is astonishing how much we dread the last darkness, while we are quite indifferent to the first.'

The child does not want to remember the frightening thing, the child does not talk about it, the child does not think about blackness, because then the blackness will begin to grow and might take the child. The child knows very well that blackness exists there even if the grown-ups look away. When the child walks in high grass so that his head does not stick out, the blackness speaks to him. It says things the child does not understand. That is dangerous because then I can't think about it, thinks the child. Behind the grass, there are juice and voices. One day I will be taller than the grass, or it will grow out of the grass and take me again.

The child will take care of himself, but when he can't take care of himself, he becomes scared and wants someone to hold him. When it is light and the grass is short, newly cut, the child thinks he is not scared of anything.

The white light. The forest floor is covered in wagtails, with their light undersides turned up. The white light. Snow covers the forest floor. The children cannot eat snow. Who is taking care that the children don't eat the poisonous snow?

The word 'zone' has become as ordinary as 'forest' or 'river'.

Becquerel

Radioactivity is measured in becquerel, which is a size that indicates the number of nuclear upheavals per second. The nuclei will stabilize in radioactive substances when they emit surplus energy as radiation. The radioactivity will therefore gradually die out. The time it takes before the number of radioactive nuclei are reduced by half of the original number is called the half-life or physical half-life.

There are short-lived radioactive substances, with a half-life of seconds or minutes. There are also long-lived radioactive substances, with half-lives of up to several million years.

In the forest, the mushrooms begin to rust. A layer of reddish iron dust spreads over the vegetation. It gradually works its way in. You can see the layers become a little thicker each day. Every time you walk here, the forest has become more iron-studded, gilded. There is no longer much underfoot, you walk on carbon steel – knives could be made out of stuff like this. You steal fruit from the trees and your teeth grate against the taste of iron. The molars devil themselves out of the mouth and get scattered like chalk from the jaws. The taste of metal in the mouth mixes with the taste of blood – metal with metal, blood iron with armaments iron. Body and corpse. You spit bits of metal and bite toothlessly, wearing a smile that become ten years older in two minutes. Don't steal apples! No! Must remember that. You go along the iron path, your heels clicking against the steel, and it smells of nails. This is how it is to be young in a new country, a country covered over, a fossilized beetle. Like Pompeii. It isn't normal. It just seems so harmless, another carpet of iron – we can surely tolerate that as well, you would have thought. But the mouth aches; where the teeth should have been, there is only air left. You hang up your maps in the middle of the room, move some stones into the living room and make a ring, a campsite. It does not look metallic, but it will be. You must move them outside every day. It will become harder and harder to find ordinary stones now, but you still have a little heap of pebbles. You make coffee at the new campsite and sing songs with toothless breath:

> *Old land, old land,*
> *don't abandon your own man,*
> *here I sit in front of the fire,*
> *Is it more than I can bear*
> *that you cheat me with the steel?*

Afterwards, you laugh for quite a long time over the newly made-up song. It is possible to laugh without iron dust on the tongue. The mechanism in the heart is running well. You have not started wondering what is happening. You are not fooling yourself. You don't fool me.

Late in the summer after the accident, I went past a woman who was selling apples from her garden in a market in Kiev. The sign at her stall said 'Delicious Chernobyl Apples' in large letters.

'But, my dear lady, do you actually sell any?'

'Indeed I do. People come a long way to buy a juicy apple for their mother-in-law, or a big red one for the boss.'

That's Ukrainians for you, I thought... And I have told this joke many times now. And to think that in those days I could not afford Chinese canned food. God only knows what was in the sausages I ate from the shops.

Olenka laughs. She has been laughing ever since the accident. A laughter that pops up when she can no longer water the petunias and tomatoes with collected rainwater. Then she laughs for a long time. She is alone – laughter alone is laughter without heart or emergency supplies. Olenka wants to stop laughing, but she can't afford to. The others hear her laughter all day. Now and then somebody joins in. They laugh at Olenka and at the situation. Many have exhausted all their tears. Laughter fills their stomachs, just as raw turnips fill one's stomach but cause discomfort afterwards. Olenka thinks she is stupid, that she only laughs a stupid laughter. The doctor says he doesn't treat laughter, and that she must control it. But suppressed laughter is a hard egg in the stomach, it is like indigestion and food-rationing. Olenka laughs every day, from when she gets up until when she grins in her sleep. Olenka works in a factory. The things they make have become laughable. They threaten to give her notice if she does not stop guffawing. Then she will be able to laugh all day. 'Die, abandon reason – or laugh', Olenka reads somewhere… and guffaws. The membrane of laughter is more fragile than tears. The laughter is a corpse smell in the mouth, like old milk. There are no lamenting women but laughing women here. Wild with laughter, Olenka winds it around her fingers. Her stomach is full of turnips, which will not lie quietly. Now and then come little jokey hiccups. The storeroom of laughter is in disorder when the postman comes with her dismissal notice. Olenka wraps a headscarf around her jaws and the cold grimace disappears in the brown cloth. Olenka tries to speak through the cloth. She can't see herself in the mirror. She looks like a train robber, and laughs until she farts.

The sweatstains under the arms are showing, the clothes are glued fast to wet, stuck-together hair – I know I smell. A woman by the spice shelf looks at me. Her trolley is full while I haven't managed to put anything into mine. She wrinkles up her nose. She has smelt it. She can surely see that I am flinching at her stare. Oh, that was a smile, a fleeting sneer. I can't bear it. Soon she will begin to laugh and get the others to join in. I smell, I must stop the smell, otherwise people will begin throwing up around me, especially those in the queue for meat; they will lose their appetites, however hungry they are for dinner. I run over to the soap shelves and try to find a deodorant. This is it, a red one, certainly for women. The smell must go away. The deodorant's cap is stuck fast under the price tag. The sweat is on its way into my eyes by now, but now I will manage it. I slip the wet stick under my sweater. It smells of flowers, roses. I rub it on, feel how sticky and disgusting it is. Why is my body so repulsive? I pull the deodorant out of the tight sweater and see several long black hairs stuck to it. I throw up. The woman who stared at me calls the shop manager. He tells me to wipe it up and says I am reported for shoplifting. Shoplifting? The woman over there said you stole a deodorant. Is it the one you have there? Yes, but I was going to pay for it. It is not allowed to try it beforehand, he says, and takes me by the arm. On the way to his office, I see the woman still staring at me. I feel a red mist in front of my eyes, hear the pulse beat in my temples, in my ears. I did it for you, I shout. It was for you I dived! I saved you all, you destroyed me! I swallowed heavy water, that's why I smell. Shouldn't you thank me? Instead, you sneer, wrinkle up your nose and go home. It was I who did the dirty work. I saved you all, do you hear? The shop manager leads me away. I have begun to cry. Snot runs down into my open mouth. I can't remember how to close it. My whole face is dissolving.

I sit on a chair. Someone hands me a cloth. I don't want to wipe away the rest; there must be something left of my face. Why do you talk like that? The man in front of me looks serious. What talk, I think, I am weeping my face away. That you were with them and dived to save the groundwater, that you went under the floor of the reactor, why do you say that when it is not true? He looks at me, not sternly, but sadly. I become sad too. He looks at what was my face – imagine what it looks like. Why? He says again. Did you do it for money? The reactor floor, the water... I see it all in front of me. I see myself diving for a red deodorant.

The man follows the fist into the other one's face, falls and falls. The fist, the man like the tail of a comet, the layer of flesh, knuckles, teeth, mucus. He has warm hands, everyone comes to him. The fist is in a dream. There are people around all the time. The little living room has been made into a waiting room. He receives them in the bedroom. When he lays hands upon someone's throat, the swollen thyroid gland bulges upwards against his hands. When they come with their skin covered in spots, he simply strokes them lightly. There is nothing else to do, the spots will not go away. But now and then they stop growing. He receives gifts from those who have something to give, things he will never have any use for, but cannot throw away, for they would see the next time they come. He likes those illnesses best that do not stem from the accident – fractures that will not mend, backache, ear infections, gastric flu. He is often ill, but his hands only work on other people. When he was small, he would stop the blood from the wounds of his playmates. He was never allowed to join in war games, it would have been unfair if he took sides. When he is ill, there is never anyone who cares; they just become sour when they have to turn back, when the curtains are drawn. Nobody knocks and asks if he needs anything.

The wolfdog comes every full moon. He knows he is dangerous,
he frightens himself. He has the eyes of a dog and the hair of
a man. You may sit on his back, and he will run over plains
where there should have been woods. He eats pieces of uranium
as big as cannonballs, he shines. The sound runs before him,
he runs after his own sound. He wants something from you,
he wants to shine for you, he wants to eat the shining in you.
Pieces of uranium fall off his back. They are the shape of stars,
stars falling on the ground. You can follow the stars and you
can run after his howling. He knows who you are. He knows
and snarls. He will obey you if you wish. He will eat you if
you wish. You can wait for him. He waits for you.

Dynamo Kiev are playing at home tonight. Shall we go over and watch? They are bound to play well. I've heard that the coach from the national team will be watching this match. Just think of that! Roman's expression is eager, he lowers his voice: You never join in anything like this any more, it's just you and Julia and the kid now. I look at him – longish tousled blond hair, seven kilos overweight in tight trousers and a much too short jacket. We have never been friends. Hung around together, of course. There are few people you spend more time with than those you were with in kindergarten and school. The bus journeys there and back, the swimming lesson days, sports meets all over the country. He notices my reluctance, but he keeps trying. I jump into his stained Volga. We're going to Kiev to watch football. I say I must phone first. Julia must get a message. She gets so upset otherwise, always imagines the worst – sirens, the foreman calling at our home, maybe a priest as well. That's Julia. I don't want this, I want to go home, but Roman is cheerful, drives on and says he knows of a telephone kiosk on the way. I know he is lying, why don't I say anything? It isn't worth it, I want to go out. Julia will only look at me, she has stopped nagging; I could stand the nagging better. It smells of old bananas here inside the car. I look around. Outside, the apricot trees are white, scattering on the windscreen. Roman uses the windscreen wipers to remove the apricot blossom. Dynamo Kiev, I don't remember the name in the first eleven in 1978, I don't. Roman is going to try out again, but the only thing I see for myself is the reserve bench. Reserve. Now I think maybe it was an honour to be nearly good enough for Dynamo Kiev, even if just for that season.

Roman is too drunk to drive home. The Volga's steering is heavy and the first gear doesn't work. When we get to the edge of town, it is morning. The roads are closed. I try to pass a bottle with a banknote around it to the watchman. He asks if we are crazy, says that he has saved our lives by not letting us in. Radioactivity is a word that wakes Roman up. He has an afternoon shift at Reactor Four today. He sits up. I know a way, we'll go in there!

The corridor is dark. After the accident, Mother refuses to use more electricity than necessary. The bathroom is at the end of the corridor. I must go there and do my hair before I go out with Roman and the others. There's light in the bathroom. Strange, I thought Mother was washing in the cellar. It has been quiet for such a long time now. The light comes out like a wedge into the black corridor, the door is ajar. I am about to shout that I want the bathroom now, it's my turn, I'm going out, you aren't. Something stops me, a whimper maybe. I peep in. Mother stands naked to the waist, her dress rolled down, and the ugly skin-coloured bra around her midriff. She is thinner than me. One arm lifted up, she rubs and strokes an area in the armpit towards the back. In the mirror, I can see what she sees but not what she feels. Her face is white. She lets her arm fall and remains standing, looking at herself in the mirror. I hide myself at once. When she has washed her face and cleared her throat ten times, she comes out. I stand behind Father's coat, which she could never bring herself to pack away.

Mother, I say. She does not answer.

Wave at the girl, so we'll have another beer, okay?

Yes.

I have thought about it for a long time. It was good talking with you, Osip.

(...)

No, well, it's like it was before, uncertain.

(...)

I have given myself six months, the hospital says more. But they hope I am right. Then they won't have to pay me more sickness benefit, ha ha.

(...)

(...)

Yes.

(...)

Bitter? No, one can't be like that. But some mornings, yes... well, yes, I am. There's something about a person's decline that makes it easier to forgive. I don't know. Nobody wants to die. I've started dreaming that my mother shoots me, every night, with a pistol. There's something or the other in that.

In any case, I'm going to eat meat on my bread every day until it's over. I've decided that.

(...)

I would have liked to see Egypt. The Nile, The Valley of the Kings. Of course, I have seen it on television.

(...)

No, that's not it... But when we are born where we are, and things turn out as they did...

Yes.

I saw the red light that night, the cloud that rose up like a mushroom over the reactor roof. I think I realized it all then.

Oh, there are many things that could have been different, Osip.

Pyotr and I have discussed it many times. The best people died or went away, only the weak stayed behind, those who were of no use even to the authorities. It is like under the collectivization in the twenties, the depopulation of villages, when the brains and money were to go into the towns. I could never have been a fireman, not everyone has what it takes. But it should not have been unimportant whether I lived or died. No more doctors come to town, even though nearly everyone here is ill. Those who aren't able to work get no help. One of the worst effects of radiation is passivity, the apathy that sits on the hands; you can't raise them up, grip the spade or fondle the cat. The cells age noticeably. Now I have talked so much that my tongue has gone numb. I can't accept that this is a punishment. What are we being punished for? We were struck down once before, during the War. I don't believe in punishment, I believe in freedom. After the accident, we have no longer had any choice. I have stopped drinking spirits, I have begun paying attention, taking notes when Pyotr and I meet. I try to remember, but what is memory and what is myth. We have created so many myths about it all. I'll stick to the facts, that's what they'll get.

You are a little too pretty to stand in a bar, you are. Do you have another coffee, or are you too tired of a bitter man, old before his time, and yet, young between the legs?

The coffee is warm. She must sit down and feel that she's at home, that it is quiet. She took two cut amaryllis flowers from the shop, two that came out too early and had become a bit floppy. She can keep them in the window, share them with the people who pass by. Those who live opposite will see that she has flowers, that she tries to decorate, that there are pretty things.

The yeast crumbles in her hands. She likes that feeling. It is almost like fingers in the seed bag. She kneads until she groans, pats them into shape and bakes the bread. She has hidden a little cheese for the first hot slices, so it can melt in that delicious way. She is saving up for a new coat, full-length, 'beige' as they say in France. She will wear it on the way to work and back, and when she goes out to buy onions and turnips in the market, and if she is asked out.

It is boring to stand in the warehouse, you don't see any customers there. But it is nice unpacking flowers and seeing what colour they are. She waters and puts them in the window. Inside her head, runs a silly song she can't remember the words of, only a melody line, over and over. She opens a new case and peeps at the plant inside. It sticks its neck out, has so many more leaves on the crown and a quite special colour, milky, with indigo, steel-grey. She stares at it, it is splendid. The stalk is straight and strong, and the flower so big, it looks like all flowers and none – a mutation, an improvement nobody could imagine. I am the first one to see it. Maybe they will name it after me. Deep inside, it has long yellow stamens, like in a heart-shaped lily. It sprinkles onto her fingers, the saffron. She licks it up, feeling the thin, pale green leaves… Someone will paint this, write poems about it.

It must have got to five o'clock without her noticing it, because now the boss comes in and shouts at her: Finish up quickly! I can't afford to pay you an extra penny and you know it. See, you put your coat on at once – ready to go, aren't you? Let's see. The boss discovers the milk-blue flower and goes quiet. What is this, how has this turned up here, was it among those you unpacked? She says: Yes, do you see how pretty it is, how beautiful? The boss glares at her. Pretty? She picks up the flower, tears it out of the pot, tears the leaves, pulls off the root that falls onto the floor, and stamps on it. Beautiful? I'll give you beautiful. This is the devil's work, Chernobyl's – this is a monster. Everything from Chernobyl must go; if we let it loose, it will win. You fool, don't you understand anything? Nothing beautiful will ever come out of the accident. Throw the rest into the rubbish. Make sure you don't drop any leaves on the way. Now, good evening.

Liquidators, they were called. Those who were up on the roof of the reactor and worked in ninety-second shifts, without proper protective clothing. Definition of friendship: To take two extra shovels with the spade to clear away the pieces of uranium on the reactor roof, so that your best friend would get away with two shovels less.

Today there is talk about who are the genuine clean-up workers, who deserve pensions, and who are cheating to get privileges.

—

Automatically she tilts her head to one side. I watch the way she poses as she waits for the flash. There is something unconsciously rehearsed about it. She must think she looks prettiest like that. In the background is Reactor Four, three kilometres away. The photographer, probably her husband, can get the tower in as well if he steps back a bit. But to get her in is more important. She smiles into the lens. The tourist bus motor has started, they must move on already. Go home and burn their clothes – get rid of them.

—

The tourist in the cafe looks different. He gazes down into his coffee cup. I say hello, but he does not look up. It will be nice to get to speak a little English again, I haven't done that since I finished university. The bartender says the man is Dutch and is staying over at the hotel, that he had gone drifting, walked about in the zone. I smile, sit down. He does not smile but does not look as if he wants me to go away. Hello, I say, good place, good coffee at least. I laugh a little. Yes, better than in Minsk, he says drily. Cheaper too, blast me if I didn't have to pay thirty dollars for a room there. Is there much about us in the newspapers, I ask, or is Chernobyl forgotten now, become a tourist attraction? I say it with a smile to show it is ok about tourists. He looks up: I don't read the newspapers, he says lightly. Do you believe in black magic? he asks suddenly. Could Chernobyl be the work of the devil? I don't know what to say. Black magic? I thought we would talk about films, travel… I drink all my coffee at once and get up to go. Nice to meet you, he says as I leave.

I must remember to fetch the medicine for Grandmother, I have delayed too long already… Shouldn't have gone into any cafe, she'll smell smoke on my jacket. What was I imagining him to be – Prince Charming? Grandmother, have you been waiting? Look, here is your medicine. Well, I think I'll go and lie down for a bit. I don't feel quite well… No, no, nothing serious. No, are you crazy, I didn't meet anyone. Really, no one at all.

I worked as a journalist for a year in St. Petersburg, and was supposed to look for stories about heroes, about events, which are recognizable and touching.

I met Anna by chance at a bus stop. An old woman with a lived-in face, I remember thinking that the photographer would have an easy job. I asked her if she remembered the siege, she looked at me. Would you like to talk about it? We are making a news story, I said. I will treat you to lunch, I went on, and pointing towards the good restaurant on the other side of the street, I took her by the arm. Afterwards

I thought that she never said yes, just allowed herself to be pulled along by someone with a stronger will, someone with a nose for sensation, someone who could smell blood from a long way off. After the meal, she began to tell her story. Her face, I tried to see for myself the eighteen-year-old she was talking about. She was freshly in love. It was wartime out in the world, but nothing could go wrong. Valentin was there. Then came the attack in 1941. Valentin was a medical student and was called up... I didn't find out that I was pregnant until afterwards. It could have happened on the very last evening... I was scared and happy. I lived by myself in a poor area, learning bakery. I wanted to be a pastry chef.

Special cakes, decorated wedding cakes. That was how I met Valentin... He came to buy bread. He came again and again, and I soon understood that he came to meet me; nobody eats that much bread. Gradually there was less and less bread, to bake, sell or eat. Corn supplies ran out. We couldn't get wheat. We could see people were hungry. On the way home from the bakery, I met beggars, men who stared avidly at my bag of bread. I gave it away, I gave away what I needed. In the end, I did not have the energy to go to work. Mummy came to visit. She brought food. That was what saved us, me and the baby. It was easier to get hold of food out in the countryside, easier to access milk, potatoes, pickled gherkins. I couldn't go home with her, I had to wait for news of Valentin. What if he came home and didn't find me there?

Ugly rumours began to spread, cats and dogs disappeared, and the rats. People were desperate... It was winter, we were cold, but the hunger was worse. Some rumours said that people who lived on the streets disappeared, but we didn't believe… A boy never came home from the park, a six-year-old girl… I couldn't believe it. Humans don't eat humans… Then we are no longer human but animals, beasts of prey…

Then I gave birth to a little boy. It was late in the winter. A little, little boy. I gave him the name Viktor. Victory… I had hardly any clothes, but Mummy came with towels and nappies and milk. I heard nothing from Valentin, had no address at which to write and tell about the cleft chin, exactly like his…

I was just going down in the backyard to empty the rubbish can and the toilet pot, and I stood there for a while. For the first time in a long time it was sunny… I thought I would run down to the shop at once. The baby was sleeping so soundly. I thought maybe I'd run down and be able to get a bit of cheese on credit. I remember it was cheese I wanted to get… so strange. It was exactly then that the neighbour came into my room and found Viktor… Maybe he strangled him at once, or did he wait a little, till he carried him to his own room?

They found the legs, a little skeleton in pieces, slaughtered, the hip joints crushed to get at the marrow. He had tried to burn the legs in the stove, but they were found… and buried. Little Viktor was given a grave.

The tears fall. Anna weeps quietly and painfully, says that she can see it in front of her even now, the little cooked legs, remains of hair, her baby eaten up, cooked into soup. The police vomited when they found the bag of frozen meat hanging outside on the neighbour's veranda. Anna speaks faster now, with more emphasis. She tells how she lost her reason, simply howled, no matter what anyone said to her. She howled day and night. She was given injections by the doctor so she could sleep, but she wailed in her dreams too. She was sent home to the village, and was not in the town when peace and Valentin returned. Four years later, when at last she had recovered enough to go back to St. Petersburg, he had married someone else. She could not tell him about little Viktor. She had no right to destroy his sleep as well. She went by herself to the grave. It looked different from how she remembered it.

Anna cried so much that the restaurant staff began sending me looks that suggested we ought to go. What could I do? I had my deadline in a few hours and had got my story. I took her arm and went with her to the bus stop again, gave her my roubles and thanked her. Then, at last, she looked up. She said: That little boy of mine, I had no more. Write about how humans can be, how they can become. A beast of prey that eats the offspring of its own race. I had to tone down the very worst of it, the editor insisted... otherwise people would gag on their breakfast coffee. I have never been able to forgive myself for just leaving her there, at the bus stop. Now the journalists come here. For them, I am a 'Chernobyl person'.

Something is forgotten. Forgotten animals, forgotten rye plants, forgotten sandy soil, forgotten groundwater, forgotten generation. It does not help if you die. It will continue after you. It carries on in your genes. Do you hear? There is no sense in your sacrifice. God looks differently at things: There must be a catastrophe before we beg. The accident is a proof of God's existence. We beg: Do you have to see it, our blood? Our blood has become bright and invisible. Look! Look anyway. The fist and the cross. Pray for us. Negotiations don't get anywhere with God. Pripjat was a town built without a church. The town that repudiated God.

In the early days, I was obsessed with revenge, frothing and spitting in the party secretary's office. At last, I was not even allowed into the building. I tried to pull the security guards by the hair, then the whitecoats came and gave me an injection. I remember I dreamed about him, swathed in rosy morphine, as he was when the telephone rang. We sat eating, the youngest one had fallen asleep at last. We were going to relax. I remember he still had the table napkin tucked into his shirt collar when he picked up the phone. I saw how he went white. He straightened himself up and began taking off his good shoes while he still stood at the phone. Handsome. My husband. The last time. I have a Caucasian temper, which gets aroused when it has to. Like when I found out that he went to her. Not to whores, but to her. I spied on him, saw him go in, go out. Saw her standing in the window, with raven hair and a white towel wrapped around her breasts. I could have killed him. He came back to me, but I will never forget. They will never get me to forget Chernobyl either, no injections are strong enough. I fight for my children, for him who was sacrificed for nothing. They talk of cannon fodder in wars, this was worse. We looked up to the scientists as gods, now they are sitting naked on the hill, helpless. Even Gorbachov, that prick, has begun speaking ill of them. Three of the reactors are still working. How can we be witnesses to this? The children. I have two. Two little ones. Fatherless before they turned ten. I will do this. Blacken them, those who are responsible. Stop nuclear power plants in the Soviet. In the world! I am strong. My children shall not die.

After the accident, he became strange. He wouldn't talk to the rest of us, just sat inside the flat. At last we had to arrange food for him, food and other necessities. Before the accident, he was a chemist, no, physicist. Maybe he knew too much. But he never said anything. He did not change his clothes until somebody asked him to. He had worked in Moscow. It was something secret. Nobody knew exactly, but he may have felt he had been let down, as everyone did. It always took a long time before he opened the door when we rang the bell. It was as if he was hiding something. He had a laboratory; one of the rooms had been converted, the carpenters told us. With time he got sicker. It was leukaemia, but he did not want to be treated, did not want to go to a hospital. We took turns visiting him, all the neighbours on the staircase. He was never grateful, maybe he wanted to die in peace. Before the accident, he was an ordinary neighbour, helped out with painting the stairway and changing windows. He received heavy parcels by post, nearly every day. There was no sender's name on them. He took them in quite calmly, but he waited for us to go, that was obvious. Naturally one gets curious. When Galina found him dead that morning, we all went into the laboratory. The key to it was in his pocket. He had become stiff, his body was still sitting up, even when we moved him from the chair onto the bed… Not a pretty sight. The locked room was full, with objects lying all over the place. He had been constructing something, something large. It was only afterwards that we found out it was a sort of atom bomb, that it was nearly ready to use… that it had a button.

Mother drinks. It would have been better if it was Father doing that. Her hair smells of vomit. Someone walks about inside the TV. What is on the surface and what is inside, how to tell the difference. You can see it in a cake, the crisp brown crust and the soft stickiness inside, but in water, in a person…? She swaps away the rations of flour for country liquor, no longer bothering to hide it. She cries and abuses me, that hurts. She is the child I speak patiently to. Wisps of hair, grey-brown, droop over her eyes that have lost their colour, running over like thick liquor. Her pores, large and open, like chopped-off wheat straw left over in a field after threshing. Alcohol is worse than strontium. She does not speak any more, though I can see her lips moving, maybe engaged in interior monologues. She's thirsty, always so thirsty. And now and then, it goes in the reverse order – vomit, spit, words. Curses, but also other things. She suddenly remembers that she is Mother, that I am vulnerable, damaged by alcohol. She was already drinking when she was carrying me, but much less. After the accident, she went through the roof. Father can't be bothered to talk to her any more, their relationship is exhausted. The lies, stained panties, the mouth that wants to meet his own, the smell… she gets hurt. I don't feel any respect, I don't know what respect is – it is a word from books. I will not cook, wash the dishes, fetch wood, stand in a queue, empty her chamber pots, wash her. I don't know which is worse for Mother, to be touched, or that I can't bear to do it. The cloth wipes lightly. Lets the smell stay there. The smell and the clinking of bottles are what I hate the most. The smell can't be talked away, not that smell. I know what people say when they hear her shouting from the balcony right out in the street. Let her fall down, fall down. God, I mean it. I will kiss her forehead a hundred times, feel how cold it is. She who said Anya-nanya-tanya is somewhere else, camouflaged. Nobody pushed, the balcony door is locked now. I just light a lamp, souls shall go wherever they like. Promise me that you will remember the little things. The blue nightdress with helicopters on it, the one you were not allowed to throw away. I see you are floating. Is it good to be so light? A different kind of elation, I have given you that… So lightly you are flying. The stomach is your stomach again, and the face smiles a smile. You are happy I did this. You were waiting for the signal. The jump was in your feet, they just had to be reminded that they could float instead of stumble. There will be pathos in the funeral oration. I wrote it already, long ago. Did you know that?

The worst is the little moan afterwards, when the jet has finished coming in a spurt, by fits and starts. The night pot is made of zinc and it is audible here. Like paper. It is worse for me, it is my mother. Stanislav tries to laugh, whispers: Do you think we can be heard just as well up in her room when we… I push him away. Stanislav talks too much, asks questions, gets no answers, still keeps on asking. They were in a hurry during her last caesarean and ripped her bladder. Now she is on the pot every half hour. We weren't supposed to live here. The flat was expropriated to a government employee. We were not allowed to leave Belarus, and Mother was weak even then and brother Mitya so small.

I don't trust myself. You can jump out into the road in front of the brown buses and become a soft stone for the right front wheel to run over. Stanislav says the accident will open up the Party, that it must happen now, that the

West will go along with it, measure radiation and emissions, calculate cancer rates. We can't hide things in the same way as before, they will soon understand that in the Kremlin as well. And then we will get a flat, or permission to go out of the country. I dare not have children here, what if they... I have no confidence any more, no confidence that it can get better. Brother Mitya can't stop running, up the stairs, down the stairs, up the stairs, and down. He is showing off for Stanislav who isn't looking at him. Brother Mitya is squashed flat in the face, so flat that the eyes are not even. They are grey and wry. He was born in the autumn after the accident. I remember how Mother bathed in the river then. That was the only thing that eased her varicose veins. She said she saw Father at the bottom of the river... Father, like a flat stone in a current. I waded into the river and looked for it once, even though I knew the water was dangerous. I wanted to see what she saw. I could have sworn that there were big black beetles with dragon's tongues, miniature monsters from another time, fetched up now when everything was on its way down. Brother Mitya wants to go for a walk. Stanislav goes into the bedroom to read a letter he has received. Don't disturb me, his shoulder says. Brother Mitya is already dressed to go out. We walk over the bridge, the cars drive fast here. I could have jerked him with me into the road, he is so light... And how will he look after himself later, with that face, and when Mother dies...? Will we have to take him in? What about going abroad? He will be like an exhibition dummy marked 'Chernobyl'. He grips my hand tightly. I run across to the kiosk to buy him a double ice cream. Have you heard, shouts the man in the kiosk, haven't you heard, troops have gone into the Kremlin, but Yeltsin has prevented the coup! The fall of the

Soviet empire! We'll get to see the fall of the Soviet empire, believe me, now right in front of our eyes – it has begun. I buy ice cream for Mother and Stanislav as well in order to celebrate. Mother is up in her room. Her hair smells of piss when she bends forward over the ice cream, grey piss. I feel nauseated and run down to look for Stanislav. How happy he will be. I shout, but he is not in the living room. I think about the brown buses, the wheels, the metal spokes that go round. There is a note in the bedroom. I am going to M. To Moscow!

The washing-up water must be over pasteurizing point. She is particular about that. The bacteria lie like hovering dust over everything here. Coughs, sneezes, sweaty handshakes – everyone is sick... She does not know anybody without any problems. The muscles in her back go into a spasm. It is anxieties she is washing away.

Even the way he knocks on the door is not boring. Before she has turned round his arms are around her, holding where they shouldn't hold. But she thinks she is laughing. One of his hands grabs hold of the bottle of juice standing on the counter and pours the contents into the washing-up water. It becomes blackcurrant froth. Vitamin C is needed for the winter, we can't drink the colour. The cups get sticky sweet. She wants to hit him. Has he no respect for her hard work, uneasiness and sleeping problems? He sees he has gone too far. They become two lopsided lovers and soap-juice. Do you see that the froth is beautiful too? He asks whispering into her ear. Laughter is vitamin too. That's what you'll get from me all winter, if you will let me. Will you let me?

Mother has pins in her mouth, she is looping up the skirt. It should be shorter at the back, for that is modern. The scent of nail polish still stings the mucous membranes in the nose. Mother cries, but she is helping. I have never cried. Why should I start now when Boris is dead. It is smiling that's needed. It is going to be difficult to buy coal for the winter. We need potatoes, and the child needs proper food.

- Shorten the dress a little more.
- Your father would have died and Boris…
- But they are dead. We who are living must survive.

She pricks herself with the pin in her mouth. Small drops of blood fall on the black material and melt. I catch one and taste it. I have to go out somewhere and dance. Not where the workers sit, those who survived their stay in the hospital in Moscow. Those who didn't survive, they are gone. My husband is gone. I have to go out. I'll go to a place where the officers and Party officials drink.

- Mother, hurry up with the hem. I must go, it's late. If the little girl wakes up give her the gruel. I still have a small waist, haven't I?

In the bathroom, black pubic hair still lies in the washing, but Mother will not see it. Maybe she has seen it already, maybe the dress has become so short that everyone can see. I'll manage it, I'll manage this. I am not dead. Since Boris died, can I let myself down? The gruel is as thick as slime. Let's hope she doesn't wake up. It is so heavy here, we can't afford to air it. Outside, the cold will come and breathe under my dress.

- See you, Mother. Don't wait up for me.

- My child, you can stay here then.
- I have gone long before, and you are relieved after all, I know that. Just take care of the child, won't you?

Red smoke all over the room. I feel my cheek. A long stiff hair in the mole. They are going to see it. Or maybe not. It's too late. I'll dance with a rich one. Dance till he can't manage any more.

He gropes and then does not. *It* knows where it wants to go, but he is unsure. I help it in. It slides. It is not dry, it is deceptive. I want it, a bit. The flat of the back is tense sweat, licked rough tongue, rough back, licked hair, nape, lower lip, cock, cock, stomach rumbles, laughter... He caresses me. The fingers are not radiation-damaged like *his*. He. He is dead. I am coming.

- So much.
- You are worth it.
- Shall we meet again, another place?
- Another place, where nobody can see us, or knock on the door.
- I'll come. Thanks.

My face is not mine. I can't think. Is he dead, is he healthy, is he here, what am I doing here? Stride. Stride. Summer like a helicopter on the roof going away. It is not I who am me. The little girl, and Mother, they know, I won't be able to forget. For coal and potatoes... It is a long time yet until winter. It feels like there's water in my brain. It runs from side to side, doesn't find a level. I smell of fear.

God is a happy cloud, Mitsya says this to everyone he meets. We must be grateful we were saved. It's getting better, don't be afraid. Mitsya is preserving humour and sense when he insists on this. That is why he says it all the time: God is a happy cloud. The winter is harsh, Mitsya is out walking the icy roads near the zone. He feels fine, sings to himself, thinks that everything is easy when one has the right attitude, therefore he must try to find more and more people to share it with. This thought puts him in high spirits. He takes extra rapid steps and falls, hitting a lump of ice. Mitsya knows it is death, as sure as the Czar. He keeps lying there. When he tries to get up, he sees that the lump of ice is bleeding.

How can my eyes be mine after what they have seen? Has my mouth anything to do with words, the shape of O and breath? The taste of sour drops rasps my tongue, my spit is blue. I dare not look at my hands. To be related to one's nose, Grandmother's nose, Father's, brothers' and sisters', nephews' and nieces', black and white pictures on the living room wall, myself? How is it to be hungry in the stomach of an animal, reduced to meat, to the flower that grows on your grave, fertilized with guts, arms and wounds?

If I climb even higher, you will be able to see under the soles of my feet. I had no dolls and lost a child, I drink water in the shadows, it creaks, I won't die before you wake up. On a lily, a lily. Shiny paper angels when God is out drinking his vodka.

How can heaven be for the good? Farewell is the favourite word, remember to forget that.

The violin that plays you, hush, do you hear? The light you shed is a lie. The finger where the ring was snapped. You may admit whatever you like. The suitcase stands half-full by the door. I can make a beggar the Czar. Go home when morning comes. The fool is us. I just give an answer. I am on the inside of the bookcase, I lick dust and frost, washed down with heavy beer. Who screamed? Can one separate the screams, voices, degrees of fear? You screamed beautifully, always. Come, let me blow on your fingers.

You look as if you want to be in an accident.

The sound of sex when you phone. On the far side of intoxication, you keep speaking loudly in an assembly that has become quiet long ago. The top hat at the side of the writing desk, a cigarette and artificial sunflowers.

A little goldfinch, which cheeps. Jam, jam, jammy.

The love poems were never out of fashion here.

One hunts a beast and catches a human.

The insect speaks, its tongue curls up between its mandibles. You understand so very well what it is saying.

It says 'maximalism', it likes m, m, m, m, m, m, like in 'mammy'. This time it says it

like always. You, for always. This. Facet-eye you think, and pinch together. A whole cow-manure. Gluttony

as in food, as in vomit.

Fly now, fly.

The well-known sign of love. The signal, the smile that otherwise is absent. Tired bodies, familiar movements in harmony. Yet, always something new. A rougher thrust, tongue in the ear, where has he learnt that? From a book. Don't think, just feel, and gradually open up. The moisture lubricates, opens, feels him. Think that the penis is a heart… pump, pump, not blood but semen. The air is used up, then reused, his breath is in my lungs. Know that the little window is all covered in dew now. The scent of sex, shining flesh, the sweat of lovemaking. Comfort and emptiness. Near and not near, but two bodies. The hand caresses the spine, slowly, quietly, soundlessly. The children are sleeping, the blanket is thrown aside. He is sweating so much that my stomach becomes wet. When he rolls over on the side, it becomes cold at once. Yearning, yearning, once more, just one more touch… hand over the stomach now, the hairs on his chest curling, soft, many, mine. My husband. The phrase, it suddenly becomes important to say. Maybe he does not hear, I say it anyway. Mine, my beloved. It is running, must go into the bathroom, dry it up, how much can come really. What is his and what is my fluid? He gets up, too, sits down in the living room and lights a smoke. When I come out of the bathroom, I see that his erection still has not subsided. I sit on top, resolute. Rock and sway, come… nearly. He smiles, takes another drag, and I realize that he didn't even put his cigarette down while I rode him. I laugh, a bit abashed. He doesn't know why but laughs with me, kisses. None of the children have woken up, luckily. It is absolutely quiet. We make love. Tired in another way, sleep in my arms, darling.

She doesn't know I am looking at her. Or maybe she suspects something. She leaves the ashtray for a long time. She does not tap into the many-coloured glass ashtray until more than half the cigarette is smoked, lets the ash from the cigarette go long. Graceful, but not for my sake. She says nothing, we wait. There is nothing to talk about, she doesn't interest me. Detest? When she looks at me, she is sure to suggest something. I know her so damn well, when she is bored, or testing me. It is either food or TV, maybe wine. Then I'll be caught, the wine glass will hold me firm. She'll want a deeper conversation, maybe sex. Will I have the energy to make love to her? Her breasts are still small and round. We never had any children. There were four miscarriages and an ectopic pregnancy. God, how ill she was. I was sure I was going to lose her. That time I was afraid. But now? The idea of losing her is absurd. She is robust, small but strong as steel. Another man? It could happen, but I don't think she is imaginative enough, not any more. She caught me, and then she gave up. Oddly enough, she suggests chess. I can agree to that, I am much better than her at that. Out of around four hundred games, she has won three, maybe. Max four. Suddenly I feel afraid. What will happen if she wins today? If that is the case, there has to be a penalty. Can't come up with an excuse now, even if she lets herself be fooled. Did I love her once? The red lips, lipstick from Paris, that strange, staccato laughter, her interest in ornithology. How many early mornings did we not spend at the beginning of our relationship scouting for a red blackstart, or was it a black redstart... She was always in camouflage gear... Did she get me to wear those green-coloured helmet-like hats with netting? Like hell she did. Did she love me? She said so, often. Far too often, I felt. Irritatingly and possessively. She would even say it in public. It was unbearable.

Chessboard on the table. I'm quite obviously ahead, so I can begin to relax. She is really almost beautiful when she sits concentrated, as if she is working out a strategy. Hair as black as ever – I think she has it dyed, I haven't asked. The lips are in any case still outlandishly red. It is always just as uncomfortable to see her without lipstick early in the morning. I turn away. Lifeless pale lips, they scare me, make me think of death and my own mortality. I could have leaned forward and stroked that smooth hair, to feel if it was just as smooth as my fingers remember. Something or the other might have loosened up without our knowing it, the thoughts must have come after... Because my hands are already fondling her cheeks.

Anna has sat down on the jacket, her breasts stir under her sweater; nobody in the class has bigger boobs than Anna's. I must take it a bit carefully, so as not to scare her. That never pays. I stroke her hair, kiss it. The tips of her hair taste of soap, doesn't she rinse out the shampoo? There's so much I don't know about her. If we get married, I'll get to find out such things. What she looks like when she's asleep, and if she sits on the pot with the door open, surely not. But all the other things, I will be able to find out. Suddenly I feel her kissing me, hard, differently. She strokes me over the sideburns, pulls a little, moves the other hand towards my crotch. Good God, this isn't Anna! Now she is trying to pull off her sweater. Shall I get to kiss her breasts at last? She unfastens her bra as easily as anything. I could never have managed it. My hand lifts up by itself. The nipples are hard – is it because she is cold or because of me? Tarasik said once that women, he said women, not girls, get stiff nipples when they are randy, remember that, he said to me, then you can just go ahead. Randy women are best, good and hot, and willing. I take off my jacket and begin to feel down inside her jeans, it's a bit tight. Her panties are thin, next to nothing. Maybe that's what silk is. She has hair, quite a lot of hair it feels like. Dare I? She opens her eyes, looks at me, closes them again and waits. I stick a finger up, it's hot! Thanks, Tarasik, you were right. There is plenty of room... maybe I am too small... maybe she isn't a virgin. It can't be helped, Anna. Now I'm going to take you.

I daren't look at Anna. She lies on her back, looking up at the sky. Maybe she is counting the stars. I must say something. Kiss her maybe. But she looks so grown-up lying there, one boob budding. I feel I want her again. She had a good time too. She moaned, at any rate.

When we get dressed, she is very quiet. Say something then, good God! She asks if I will brush off her back, if she has dry leaves in her hair. I brush for a long time, even if there is nothing there. I want to touch her, say that... What shall I say to her? That we are proper lovers now, that we are going to be together, that she need not be afraid, the condom didn't burst any of the times. I know she could not have borne an abortion. Suddenly I feel ashamed. What have I done to her? As if she is reading my mind, she says she wanted it, too, that she had wanted it for a long time, with me. She smiles, and I feel sweet tremors run through my torso and right down in my cock. Is this love? I believe I love her, and I say it aloud to her: Anna Ivanova, I love you! She is laughing and serious at the same time, and starts to walk towards the moped. I must go home, she says, Mother is waiting, she is alone, and Father has an extra shift at the plant. It is probably something secret, an experiment or something. It is nearly half-past two when we turn in towards the town. Look, shrieks Anna from behind the helmet, look over there! She points in the direction of the plant. There is a strange light over it. A huge red and grey cloud, shaped like an enormous mushroom, is slowly on its way up towards the sky. The stars seem so small. Anna is hysterical on the back of the moped: Drive faster, drive much faster. What if something's happened to Father! When we come into the town centre, we see ambulances and fire engines all over the place. They have different sirens, but now they seem to be blending into a long, terrifying howl. Anna shouts: Drive me to the hospital at once, I have a hunch that Father is there. I refuse, say good God, you don't even know what's happened, maybe it isn't at the plant, maybe it is only a practice, calm down. She doesn't listen to me, stares wildly into my eyes for two long moments, and before I have time to move, she begins running towards the hospital. I remain sitting on the moped, watching after her.

I am glad I'm not alone in being me.

Ecological Half-life

Ecological half-life indicates the time it takes before an organism has halved the quantity of radioactive material in its tissues while living in an area affected by radiation. Animals absorb radioactive material through the food they eat and plants take up radioactive nutrients through the root system. The ecological half-life is correlated with the physical half-life and the thinning out of radioactivity through scattering in the environment.

As if in the Spring Sacrifice, we see a young girl dancing herself to death. Then we tear the puppet to pieces. The weeping women sigh over the puppet, the grass sways prettily in the wind, and the sky is a light blue that it only becomes far eastwards. The spring is not clean. I love the black tones in hair, the trace of rawness when we pull at an arm. I wanted to show this to you. Come along, dance, come with what you feel, as Grandfather Frost comes with the spring. The Snow Maiden stands watching. Dance, only dance. Do you see the bonfire? That's where we are going.

Out of the way. I must get past. Excuse me, Vasiliy shouts. He is coming with a cake and runs past the queue in the supermarket. He throws some notes at the check-out lady and runs out again without waiting for change. The cake looks like a top hat he has taken off while he is running. The cake is to go by train. The train is already at the station and Vasiliy tears along. He sends a cake to Jelena every day, and every day he is just as late. Jelena never eats the cake. She does not even open the parcel. She hardly registers new cakes from Vasiliy. He is well aware of that, just the same he has decided to send a cake every day until Jelena will have him. Jelena sucks her thumb when nobody sees and does not want to marry anyone. She looks like liquorice but certainly tastes more like caramel. Jelena wants to work in the theatre. While she is waiting to recover, she watches the way maggots eat up the raspberries. She goes for walks along the river and dreams of successes on the stage in Moscow. Without noticing, she comes quite near Pripjat. Only ghosts are left in the town now, ghosts and cats. All the cats have gone blind, they walk in the middle of the empty streets with white, dead eyes and meow for their owners. Jelena peers in at one of the windows, it is smashed. Inside on the table, stands a half-eaten, petrified lunch. Jelena goes into a house where the seal is broken. She squats on the floor and pees; with a whole box of matches, she tries to set fire to her own pee.

Jeva is in love with Vasiliy. She is a cleaner at the plant and sees him every day at work. She matches her shifts to his, she sneaks a look at the shift lists when she cleans the offices. She thinks of him when she is eating, when she is walking and when she is going to sleep. She thinks of him when she is thinking. She knows he sees only Jelena, that he sends her cakes every day. Oh, he does not notice her when she cleans around him in the canteen where he eats rye bread and drinks tea. He should eat something other than rye bread, thinks Jeva. She begins sending cakes to Vasiliy. When the first cake arrives, Vasiliy becomes very surprised. He cycles all the way to Jelena's house to talk to her. She does not open the door, just shouts to him from the veranda that he must go away. But why did you send me a cake then, he shouts back. I haven't sent any cake, you cake-man. You must have sent it to yourself, I think. Vasiliy becomes even more astonished. While he eats the cake, he thinks it must be one of his friends, or maybe it is a woman. When the next cake arrives, he meets the messenger and asks who the sender is. It is Jeva. Then he suddenly remembers all the glances in the canteen. That day he really comes too late to the train station, and stands there with a cake that has to be eaten. Maybe he should send it to Jeva and see what happens. He does that and goes uneasily to the evening shift. Jeva looks well fed. She licks her mouth like a cat. He looks directly at her, she herself has enough sense not to look his way today. Jelena notices that the cake does not arrive and understands what that means. She feels a throb behind the temple. What if she never gets into the drama school, who will look after her then? She decides to send a cake to Vasiliy. The cake is big and pink. Two cakes on the same day is a bit too much for Vasiliy, he can't eat both of them. The one from Jelena is left untouched, but he gazes at it all the time. He knows he will never be happy with Jelena, that she will harp on about the theatre, that she is very sensitive. He wants her anyway. He loves the way she looks like liquorice, that is his favourite. He knows, too, that she does not love him, that she only got scared that someone else may have stolen her suitor. He thinks he will have her, regardless.

The theatre is full of people. Jelena and Vasiliy sit in the front row. Jelena is sweating, he can smell sweat from her mouth. She has to see everything, also show that she is here, so that someone can see her. She wants to be seen. Vasiliy looks more at her than at the play. She is a theatre in the theatre, with her obvious feelings. He can't resist her, so naked and self-confident – he loves her. You are a frightened roe deer in the forest, a squirrel in too high a tree… I am climbing here beside you, do you see it? She does not see, but he can see for both of them.

Jelena comes in. She has a crooked nose. On her, that too is beautiful. She has not washed her hair, she could have done that. She has no respect for me. I have known it all the time. The bitterness comes out when she drinks. Why did it happen to us, what went so wrong? I want to go out, but my steps don't exist on the stairs.

Jelena didn't even look at me when she came in. I feel contempt, not grief. Can't tell the difference. Love is a different principle. I am afraid I shall stop myself from leaving.

Vasiliy stands watching the timber train pass by. Eighteen wagons of timber and snow. Closer to the sea, the snow will fall off and melt. The timber will be used for making boards and houses. Vasiliy does not know why, but the timber train makes him happy. The timber is forest, the timber is home. He knows how it smells. He turns around, fingering the piece of paper in his pocket. That too is tree fibre. He looks for the rings of the years, but on it is tea, bread, fruit (if they have any), potatoes, fish (if they have any). It is Jelena who has written it, carelessly tidy, like everything she does. He thinks he could have simply jumped onto that train, gone along to the sea, come back again, and gone to the forests. He thinks that there is something that holds him back: a packet of tea, fruit (if they have any), Jelena… And it is nearly Christmas too… Then he must buy a cake.

Two women sit in the yellow hall. Sisters. They do not speak to each other. They sit bent over books whose letters stand on top of one another forming a thick black column. The landscape: curves and hills with leafy trees. A hare. Between the trunks. Clouds. The clouds drift as they have drifted before, in formations that are always a little different. You could call it beautiful, but the women don't call it anything at all. They are young or middling, with thin or middling curls. Another sister phones. Scorn and fear at once in the voice. Why aren't you coming, it can't go on. Yellow is too poisonous. But they no longer pick up the phone, do not look at each other when it rings. Maybe they do not hear. But they hear. And they see. But the map does not match the terrain. The landscape is the same, but the contour lines have altered themselves. The books are heavy in their hands, the back feels it, bent forward in a bad posture. A hawk. They do not look up, neither does the one who was hawking for an effect. Oh no, they certainly don't do that. They sit with their heads bowed, enough similarity in the bowing. They could have said that now the Easter lilies out in the garden are budding, two more days of mild wind and they will bloom. They menstruate at the same time, the hormones adjust themselves. They change sanitary towels and do not laugh. Laughter has been absent for a long time. Of course, one can't blame Uranium and Plutonium for everything. That would be crude injustice. Many things were wrong before, much has become better since, and conversely. It is like being on a winter trek and suddenly finding a large circle where the snow has completely melted. At the centre, a point, a stone. You are cold, you pitch the tent. You think the stone must be warm, you take it into the tent. It works. At one time it was warmer, that was nuclear warmth. What is there to say? The women are silent, that is wise of them. Naturally. They go to fetch the post, alternately. They dust the yellow hall as before. They are not stupid, far from stupid, even if the telephone sister thinks they are idiots. There is French wine in the cellar, they can drink that when they like, but which of them will suggest it first? It can be quiet for a long time in the yellow hall, over Easter, through the summer, always. Or it can be broken now. A word is something different from a sneeze, it must be commented on, responded to. The Easter lily is already open. Must be taken in, watered, displayed. They sleep with the lights on. One Easter lily is not enough. A field of waving yellow. Puffs of pollen... scent. It is not true that scents went away after the accident. The women surely see their roles, but are they tragic or comic? There are so many kinds of laughter, and the public applaud enthusiastically. Three curtain calls, a little unsynchronized bowing, but it is only charming. The light goes out. One can go out of two doors from the yellow hall, they have one each. And in the tent, nobody is lying freezing. A forgotten programme on a spindle-back chair says there's a new performance tomorrow.

We have an old TV, it was Vitaliy who brought it. He had swapped it, god knows how. At any rate, he did not dare to keep it at home; it must have been stolen from one of the evacuated houses. He dumped it at our place, and no doubt it radiated more than advertisements. I was happy, though, for we didn't have to talk to each other. Oleksandr sat watching all the time. We let ourselves get snowed in, I thought afterwards, grateful for everything that brought calm, white calm, and talk, voices – always voices and lovely faces. We never commented, watched everything from winter sports to drama serials, debates, weather forecasts... And then the news. That was the most dangerous for a long time. But now nobody talks about the accident any more, not on the screen, not in the papers. We simply watch, and it is good that nothing about Chernobyl comes up. Oleksandr gets so angry then, grumbles for days, but the screen gets him to shut up in the end. Earlier some indignant or affirmative grunts might have been emitted if there was good music. Now even grunts have become too much. I myself like the ads best. All the blonde ladies standing talking about shampoo and catfood, catfood that looks better than what I put on the dinner table. The children who eat golden chocolate, with their fat hands around the silver foil. Fat hands, hands with dimples. Now and then there are films. Polish films are the best. Franciszek is my favourite, tall and magnificent. Once he played a retarded person, that was creepy. The TV stays on even while we sleep. We fall asleep to its sound. We should have had a remote. Vitaliy told us they exist. Oleksandr wants one, too, I am certain. I watch him when nature programmes are on… He misses the mountains. He should not have come here to work, but there was unrest in Chechenya then, and after all, nobody could have known what was going to happen here.

Food programmes are the worst. They should know better than to broadcast that kind of thing now. People get angry when they are hungry. Oleksandr can't bear to look at lamb chops with pickled beetroot on the screen. That is the only time he beats me. Food shows should have been banned… Porridge with masses of cream and real sugar… I understand that he hits out then. It is not very pleasant. I am not a very good cook. I do waste food, I admit. After all, I can't keep standing all the time in the kitchen either. A new programme is beginning on Channel Three. It's going to be good, I believe. It's just going to begin, I can hear the theme music, it is festive. Oleksandr nearly grunts, I can see it in him… And there are never two food shows on the same day.

I took with me a stone from the area around the reactor. It kept lying on the bookshelf for a long time. Now and then, I picked it up. A friend, who dropped in and got to hear where the stone came from, threw it out of the window.

﹏

She is swimming as she always does at the *dacha*. With confidence in what floats up. A tic on the right side of the lip will not give up, it jerks all by itself. After the bath, it is just as hot. Imitation leather against bare back. One thinks of expeditions to the Pole, that cold is so much better; that anything is better than this sweating. It trickles where it is not supposed to trickle. Between the fingers. And the navel is full. She hears the drips of day. An insect under a magnifying glass… She is waiting only for the nail, which will pin her down permanently into the collection. The heat that went into her head gave fever and madness. Father only beat me in the hot weather. The blows were not so painful then, his hand was always cool. Afterwards, she was given melons, warm and watery. The sound of the word 'water-carafe'… she bought one with her first wage. Later the wages went more on medicines; she had more care for the others than for her own children. They will not forgive her for that. It is no longer so hot now.

﹏

We took in the baby girl that autumn. It was a happy time. She was only three months old then. We could not see anything wrong with her, no missing body parts that rumours said were so common. She is only a little slow but so cheerful. She smiles all the time. What we did was right.

She was quiet, she always was. Did as we told her, sat in her room, smiled seldom and slightly. I don't remember her laughter. Maybe it did not exist. We were at the *dacha* over the weekend. She was to stay at home and study. When we came back by the last train on Sunday, the house seemed unvented in the heat, and dark. I did not call out to her. Something held me back. Her room was very tidy.

The fakir swallows fire. The dark women are heard on the other side of the square. It is late summer. A far too yellow half moon hangs between the trees. The choir of jugglers sings plaintive gipsy verses. We have eaten stuffed carp. The music changes. A dancer comes forward. He dances the Botho dance, the dance of pain. It is said that it arose after Hiroshima, and involves a slow, slow movement from one point to another. Besides the music, the scraping of a saw is heard. Someone sobs loudly. Some are angry, they want the fakir back, or a clown – can't anyone find a clown? The clown does not come, for he is the dancer. A girl applies nail polish, does not watch. On the stalls, baked apples with caramelized sugar are sold. There's an aroma of wild pig sausage and light ale. Now the girl is slowly combing her long hair. Then she disappears among the stalls. The laughter has come back. The clown has finished dancing and painted his face white. Autumn has arrived in that face. Maybe he has been struck, injured by fire, the face looks like that. Now he can laugh, people laugh cautiously with him. Tomorrow will be sunny, the colour of the moon has promised. We will come back and see more dancing. Not so scared now, it is our pain, too, expressed by a clown, without clown's movements or masks. I lie down and sleep. In the dream, someone says : 'This is not your dream'. It is a long time since I spoke. I don't speak when I am hungry. The girl at the fair, she with the nails and the hair, said she had several apples left, if I wished I could have two from her.

She is eating dried fruit, figs that have hidden sweetness inside themselves. The bus seats are warm, she just wants to sit here, for it is cold outside now. She is on her way to the cemetery on the memorial day. Only the graves are left where she lived before. She has food and vodka with her, to serve up according to the custom. The graves are lent time in there. She does not want to go back, but she has to. You only have to sit down in the right bus. Then you undertake something for yourself, something expected, maybe appointed.

I have waited too long, I feel exhausted even before it begins. Should have brought tea, hot, sweet, with as much milk as I like, not like he wanted it when he was alive. The dead must adapt themselves to the living.

The bus stops suddenly and turns. She must walk the last bit; she looks back at the bus driver. Oh, to have gone back with them… But then they would have looked at her, the dead. The figs are like lumps in her stomach, far too many, and too sweet for the winding roads here. The nausea has begun in her feet and goes and hides itself behind her tongue. The jaw is tight, tight. Come. Come again. You have only to walk. She is safe from his look now, it can't get at her any more. He sleeps without pain, without gangrene in his radiation-damaged legs. Gangrene. That word scared her so much. It smelled so horrible, the yellow slime, the rotten meat on a living man. He screamed so loudly when they sawed off his legs. She had stopped feeling anything for a long time, but he had to have food, water, a new shirt, bedpan, medicine. One mouth to send soup down into, another which spat it out. Yellow slime, it came up in her throat, spoke out. But who would hear? Nobody wanted to hear, everyone was happy he could be at home, so good, so right. The figs she vomited are covered with slime. Down in the snow it looks like a little nest where the eggs have been smashed. What remains are yellow lumps and white slime, no chirping of birds in the spring. She straightens up and walks along the road. It was going to be asphalted, but nothing happened, and now it never will be. This is one of the most poisonous places on the planet. A place meant only for the dead and those who visit them. Some other people have also been here today. Small footprints near the tombstones that cast shadows on the snow. The sun must be about to come out. There is the stone with *his* name snowed under. Her hand lifts itself to brush away the snow. The stone sinks again. There is no point, no reason… She does not have the energy to set everything out as for a meal. She just puts down the food and vodka, and leaves. She walks through the snow. It isn't easy. You need tremendous energy just to breathe. She sits on the snow, gazing inwards. It is not cold, it is something that resembles warmth. The bus driver yells: We'll be too late, must watch the route. He won't leave anyone behind, no matter what.

There are big babushkas in the baths. They have large abdomens, as if they have had eight babies in one go. They have black hair everywhere, some completely grey. One of them is beating herself with dark twigs. She wonders whether they have ever been sucked. She can almost imagine a man on his knees in front of one of them. Then the thought vanishes. One is talking to her, asks if she would like to sit on the highest bench. She sits and lets the hot steam float the dirt away. The steam prevents her from seeing the others. She is alone and does as she pleases.

Nina is the voice. The women say she can be something. Everyone listens when she sings. She grows and grows. Soon she is only the voice. Nina has an egg in her throat. Sometimes she dreams that she is the egg, that she is boiled and someone cuts the top off her with a knife, without her noticing anything. When Nina coughs, the egg jumps in her throat. Nina knows it, she knows that she is growing more than she ought to, but the voice is also growing with her. The women clap, the whole assembly hall claps, claps red as raspberries and late plums. The eyes grow the most, more than the voice. They are cow's eyes, like eyes painted on wooden boats. Nina's eyes are large, she sees with cow's eyes. That is the illness.

The sound of camphor drops exploding in warm tea. It will be good to be ill. Nina likes having a pain in the throat, a pain so acute that she cannot sing... Maybe she will never sing again.

I don't know whether I'll wake up again when I go to bed. Is there suddenly something that breaks? I don't know. It is good not to know. In the knowledge, I am prepared and not prepared. Now and then I forget, for quite a long time. Not that I have a fatal illness, but that I am going to die. I always played dead when I was small, lay down on the snow and stayed. The other kids lifted me up and pulled still me along on a little sledge. They would bury me in the snow then. I liked dying. I am willing still. It's just that I would have liked to live a bit longer. 'Nina made so many people happy at the concert today,' Mother always accepted smilingly when others said, 'she has the voice, she can go far.'

I cried. My hand was often quite cramped up from holding the mike too tightly while I sang.

I hear what the others are saying, that I look like an apparition... Have you heard that she threw Igor out?... And he only wanted to help... She is not the least bit grateful, she wants to be rather big about it. That she is ill is surely no more special than others being ill. We are all ill... She wasn't like this before, even if there was always something peculiar about her and the voice.

A strand of my hair falls. It makes a noise. I can't brush my teeth. They fall out. Fear is stuck between the teeth like a hair. I hiccup, violently, hiccup until I can't catch my breath. The fridge wails. I can't sit like this. How deep is a grave?

Can one smell the autumn – that smells of earth – down in the earth? It is my death, and I laugh at it if I want to.

I walk on the pavement, looking in front of me, as if in a corridor; I don't wish to meet anyone I know. The corridor narrows. At its end, stands Igor. He makes a grab at me, grabs in the air. I run into the first shop, a watchmaker's. The ticking of twenty different clocks disturbs me. Tick, here goes the time. Tock, the street does not exist. Tick, only the clocks. Tock, one clock is blue. Tick, a blue second. Tock, thanks, may I have that one?

Grapes stick in the throat, the throat can't be found. The grapes stop and then want to come up. Tiredness is a border, the eyes are too large for their sockets. I can't remember the taste of water without metal.

The skin has bobbles, like an old woollen sweater. But the fingers can't stop touching it. They run over the throat, feeling for more. The lumps that lie along the collarbone move aside under the hand. The lumps that hide along the esophagus are more dangerous, they spread themselves and consume. The fingers turn and find a sleeping tit, which has long been asleep. The fingers stroke it absently, but the tit is cold and indifferent. The fingers try to stroke out the nipples and they grow bigger. The fingers want to be kind, they want to caress where no caresses are given. Why not try to ball the fingers into a fist, a blow might be better. But the fingers will neither ball into a blow nor a blessing; they believe in white skin. The abdomen has had a visit. There are ten fingers playing over that large white expanse. The fingers comfort, stretch and smile. They are on their way back up, they have been for a visit and warmed themselves.

It is winter. The sky is turquoise. The feet are not cold any more and the blanket is steaming. The fireplace has been closed up for a long time. Everything is a practice for giving up. The room is larger and breathes, happy that there is life still, as it beats in the fingers. The pulse in the groin meets the pulse in the finger. There are no others who see, they lie sleeping. Do not know how one warms oneself in the snow. Should have just gone to sleep after that... There will be struggle again tomorrow. Sleep teases, maybe now, or now, or soon, can't manage to relax and smile. The night has other rules, night rules, winter rules, heat rules... Two hands around the tangle of hair, hard... In all this, the kiss is lacking.

Humanity cannot follow where light is so weak. I can't have her gaze at me. I can't manage to stay sad, Mother tears me apart into pieces. The discomfort in my thigh has thrown sleep out of the bed for several nights now, and I know something is going to happen. I put the fork into my thigh. Through the trousers, I can actually feel the point. What shall I say... It was a sound, a soft echo, then the scream. The street is much too narrow and I am waiting in the bus queue. I want to see some living animals. The butcher has only dead hares; the gipsies never eat hares – it is unlucky. 'Geysir' is the most beautiful word I know. The rain is a contrary motion. I think it falls upwards. It can look like that. The sludge on the window quivers. Mother should not have come, but she is coming. She wants to watch while she is losing me, but she will not be allowed to do that. I will be alone in that, that's definite. She is going to come in the evening, then she will go. So long as she doesn't cry… I have to bear that, too – we are bound together like links in a chain. My fingers are cold, and it is impossible to warm them anywhere. I have thrown away the wild pig skin gloves I got from Igor. It would have been good to have them now. Links. Iron is a good sinker. It is getting lighter. Now half the town is in sunshine.

- Nina, are you at home?
- Yes, come in.
- It's so cold in here. Would you like me to help you light a fire?
- No, I want it like this.
- That's no good. You should be nice and warm.
- No, leave it, Mum. I said, I want it like this. No need to light a fire. It's warm enough here. I have only a little coal left.
- I knew it, and that's why I brought a big sackful from home. You are not to sit here and freeze.
- No, Mum, don't do it. I've decided not to have it so warm. I must be allowed to choose for myself how I want it.
- Just sit down. I'll get out a bit of bread for us. It doesn't look as if you eat either. Why do you do this against yourself, and against us?
- Mum…
- Oh Nina, are you crying? Was it something I said, Nina, my child? Stay with me now, come home. We shall all look after you.
- I can't. I have to stay here.
- Come home. It will be all right.

164

The cafe is half-full and noisy. It is a weekday and only the thirstiest and the unemployed are out; there are hardly any women around. I feel distended, like bare branches in a bonfire from which smoke billows out. The air could be cut with a knife as they say. Something suddenly makes me fearful of knife play and fighting. People have become so resentful after the accident. Afraid and angry at the same time, as we Soviets have always been. But maybe things are going to change now. The men here talk only about Moscow and the attempted coup against Yeltsin. Is it really something new, or was it only something perpetrated by gangsters? I have drunk too much beer and too little vodka. In this crowd, it is meaningless to sit nearly sober. I can hear how everything is reeling around the ears of the men. People are more fatalistic than ever: Let's live now before we die! Live, live, cheers! The beer slops over my hands, and it is narrow like in a mink farm. Suddenly I catch sight of a young woman. It is strange I haven't noticed her before. She is so drunk I can hardly believe she got down the stairs quietly. Her dress is bright red, she is buxom, and has long brown hair. Women when drunk lose all their grace and appear vulgar. I have never bothered about them, only turned away in disgust when they've become clingy just before closing time and when I've known that the alternative is a cold bed. She tries to focus. The men go on talking, discussing whether the army should be sent in or not. Civil war. Independence. There is not much to gain from that either, so I stare at the woman. She notices me looking at her and begins moving in my direction, every step astonishingly purposeful. Strong, I think. She plumps herself down on my lap without ado, her body lighter than I would have expected. I think she hasn't had any children, for she is buoyant. Then she kisses me. A small tongue, like a snail sticking its head out, begins to make itself known in my mouth. Come on then, she says, and I get up.

Muscles twitch. I can't sleep when my teeth are clenched. And it is always cold under the blanket. Now Tanya is ill too. Cancer has become like a common cold, something ordinary we talk about. I feel the lumps but can't show them to the doctor, there's nothing to be done anyway. I talk too much, my head runs away with me, doesn't want to stop, doesn't want to think. The fear of the disease is even worse than the disease itself. The fear of becoming worse, of hearing that it will not get better. Lying in bed with folded hands. It is four o'clock, then five… It will be light in a little while. I must go to work, can't afford to lose one day's wages. I can't talk to Tanya now, she only cries, and her cries get hollower by the day. Behind the crying, there is nothing in the world. Only statistics. You and You and You. Everyone.

I slept through it all that night. When the reactor blew up into the air at 01.23, I was asleep. Now and then I wonder if I am still asleep. I remember the first time we were allowed to drink milk again. It was several weeks later, on the way to the Urals. How good it tasted. I had a bad conscience, because I had secretly drank a little radioactive milk back home. Even now I can't drink milk without feeling ashamed, sometimes I don't remember why; I just feel the disgusting cloying along with the taste of milk. Breast-feeding was horrible. I had two abortions before little Lyudmila. Nature cleans up, said my doctor, even after Chernobyl. Soon you will have a healthy child. Lyudmila is healthy. She is quiet when I am quiet. Much of the fear around my abdomen may have gone into her. My milk is not radioactive, I had it tested; I feel ashamed all the same. Anxiety sits tight in one place or another. It makes me heavy-headed, thick-throated. I tried to go back to Pripjat, the day before the fifteenth anniversary of the accident. I couldn't cope with the crowds and journalists at all. Maybe I believed it would be better after I had seen it. Reconciled. It was strange to travel from Kiev in that direction. The villages on the way had not changed: green-painted fences, with chickens behind; bright coloured houses and blossoming fruit trees. The areas around Chernobyl had been recreation spots for the whole of Kiev. People came there and fished and picked mushrooms and berries. The crown of my head is prickling, we are getting close. If I am able to feel anything at all, it will be painful, convulsive. At the thirty kilometre zone, we were stopped and had to show our papers. Then we came to the sign that says 'Chernobyl'. Hadn't seen it since I turned around in the bus and left during the evacuation. I had looked at the sign and thought we would only be away for some days. Somewhere inside me, there was a doubt; I bade a sort of farewell.

Inside the innermost ten kilometre zone. Now I can see the nuclear plant. It is flat and the reds on the tower are clear against the new green leaves. From here, it looks small. The idea that particles from this tower have reached all over Europe is unreal. We turn off before the plant and drive into the Pripjat road. Nobody has done any roadwork here for fifteen years. The car bumps and tries to swing away from large potholes. Another hundred metres and I can see my house.

This is where I lived once. This was my view. There were new houses, around old pine trees. The town was built right inside the forest; now the forest is busy taking over again. Trees are poking up through holes in the asphalt. There are bird's nests in the lampposts. The sign at the shop hangs and swings, will fall down soon. Scrub forest and lawns have grown again. There is the school. I go inside. The doors are open. There must have been animals here, boars maybe, or the hybrid wolves they talk about. Stones have fallen from the roof, all sorts of things lie thrown about. I go into the carpentry workshop. The planing benches lie there still, with the raw materials in place. Someone had homework – rough books, pens and an atlas lie forgotten. In my old classroom, there is still a sum written on the blackboard. I find my desk and sit down. There's my shelf, and a book with my name on it.

A big tree has lost a branch in the wind. It must have happened quite recently, for the resin trickles; it will not scar. I don't go up into the flat. Everyone had warned me that there was large-scale looting right afterwards; I won't find anything that isn't destroyed. Nature's building a new Nature here.

<hr />

The stone you sat on. I come here every evening now. I want to see the last thing you saw. You had chosen a time with little light. I can understand that. When the priest speaks to me, he doesn't try to explain. We talk about other things, as we talked before, before the sickness, before the accident.

I weave, make red and orange mats, send the shuttle back and forth, tug the thread tight. Three hours may have gone by when I get up. The movement calms me. The rhythm soothes me. He used to be soothed by my weaving too. I should have woven more. That first evening, his arms held me. He had long arms and he wore a blue shirt. I can hear him laugh. He laughed in the face of sadness. He made me add bright colours to the weaving.

He was called to the site for three months to clear uranium. We knew he was not strong enough, yet I waited for him to return. I hugged him at the station when he came home, even though I believed I could feel the radiation through his clothes and his skin. But it was actually his head the radiation had damaged. We bought sausages and went for a walk. We needed to get used to ourselves. He didn't tell me. I didn't really want to know either.

It is already dark, gulls circle over the river. I bend down to look for dark brown spots in the sand, but the rain that night washed away the blood. His blood has gone down into the earth. That is also a kind of burial.

You should not have gone to the zone, but then there seemed to be no choice. My smile muscles still work, that is strange. Now it is quite dark. Someone is coming this way. I see it is your mother. I will have to talk to her.

Your mother asks if you ever told me about your uncle, that he too committed suicide. You always said you didn't know whether your mother loved you. Were you sure of me? Did I succeed in getting close to you? How did we love each other? Over the stock of a pistol? I left you in peace, I thought that was what you needed. But I won't be able to go away from the stone. I want to sit here tonight with you. Your mother may sit too. She is talking about her brother. I feel like telling her that there is more to her than sorrow. The gulls understand that sometimes it must be absolutely quiet. Her shawl, which we're sitting on, it was you who bought it. You are closer to both of us now, are you looking?

She has stopped talking, that's good. Maybe she can also hear you.

We can only be reunited after death, my love. Do I believe that?

There are no insects in the room. I was afraid the flies would come and eat at you. It is cool, almost cold. I look at your body all the time. Try to notice the changes in your skin. In between I feel a bit faint. Wax, not skin. You lie so still, yet I often see you breathing. There's the memory of breath. I will move the white tallow candle, but it can stay a bit longer. Your wounds are under the sheet. Nearly black, and aching. It is you, but you are not breathing. Listen to me. My arms have not held you.

There are little people living inside the reactor. They stayed on, but nobody knows they exist. They fish in the artificial pond around the plant. Fish live in the water used to cool the reactor. They are huge fish, over two metres long; they became larger from the radioactivity. But the humans have only become smaller, a quick adaptation to the environment. In a few years, they have become exactly the right size to get into the cavities in the reactor, into the air pockets, into the passages underneath where water drains out through trapdoors. The trapdoors are difficult to move. But they are strong, these little people, stronger than before. Even though there are many of them, they don't speak to each other – they don't need to. They don't do anything together, there are no discussions ever; what would they talk about, after all? Evolution has taken away speech from them as rapidly as it gave it to them. Their vocal cords are fused, the tongue reduced, it works only to slurp in white boiled fish. Only the birds, which fly in and out of the imperfectly sealed sarcophagus, see them. If workers come inside to check whether everything is under control in the reactor's slow cooling-down process, they hide away before anyone can see as much as their shadow. It rains on them on autumn evenings, it snows on them on winter evenings. The sun shines and the moon is there too. Everything is there, but they are forgotten. People believe they died in the explosion, but they did not. They survived, and live on, and nothing indicates that they are going to die because everything functions. Their bodies are nimbler than before, more supple. They always get fish because they understand how to catch them, how the large old ones will rise up towards the light, up towards the bait, a fly maybe. And they stand out on the bridge, fishing. They get their own fish and go inside through peepholes, control doors and ventilation shafts, and boil the fish by putting it down into the reactor water before it goes to cooling, when the water is nearly boiling, but only nearly, and the fish can stay there for ten or maybe twelve minutes until it is white and detaches from the bone and can easily be sucked in.

They have brought rugs for themselves from the personnel rooms, pillows as well. And the luckiest have found torches. Once they must have been brothers, friends, sons, relatives, members, registered, interested. They must have had telephone numbers, driving licenses, trade union membership cards, places on waiting lists for flats, Party membership maybe, filofax diaries where cinema trips, working hours, parties, choir practices were recorded. Now they have nothing left to be identified by. They are alive, but nobody knows they exist.

Afterword

When I was ten years old, Reactor Four at the Chernobyl Nuclear Power Plant exploded. Vast quantities of radioactive fallout came with the wind from the east that spring. I grew up in an area in central Norway that was badly affected. We were three sisters who were playing outside on the April day when the rain brought Cesium 137 with it. My sisters had to have their thyroid glands removed; they still have scars shaped like a necklace on their throats. I wrote this book in 2001 and 2002, before and after a two-month long journey to Ukraine and Belarus. I stood close to the nuclear power plant and saw how the sarcophagus around the reactor was disintegrating.

At School No. 6 near Kiev, I noticed that many youngsters there had scars like those of my sisters'. The thyroid gland absorbs radioactivity. Iodine treatment might have helped, but the health authorities did not brief us about that. The schoolchildren in Ukraine did not get that sort of information either.

Chernobyl is still going on. People are still falling ill in Ukraine and Belarus but also in Norway. Even now the ground is condemned, even now sheep and deer have to be given clean food. The time it takes for certain radioactive materials to break down is extremely long. Chernobyl is a catastrophe that has only just begun.

I am giving this book out now, prompted by fear of the tendency to see nuclear power as a correct environmental choice in comparison with energy forms with large carbon emissions. People will never again be able to live in the zone around the plant. The frequency of mutation among the pine trees in the area has increased to 80 per cent. To play down the risks of nuclear power is to forget Chernobyl.

I have borrowed quotations and situations from Svetlana Aleksievitz's documentary book *Bon For Tjernobyl: En Framtidskronika* (Prayers for Chernobyl: A Chronicle for the Future).

A thousand thanks to Torunn Borge. Without you, there would be no book.

Ingrid Storholmen
Rome, Oslo and Verdal
March 2009

Acknowledgements

I would like to thank Mira, Marietta Taralrud Maddrell, for this fantastic translation. I'm so happy that my book and I met you. And thanks to Matsya who went through the translation, matching it with the original in October 2011 in Trondheim. Thanks also to Tom Fredrik Kjesbw who helped in making this translation as refined as possible. At the end, I want to thank Teji Grover and Rustam Singh for their friendship.

Ingrid Storholmen
Verdal, March 2011

P.S.

Insights
Interviews
& More...

....

Chernobyl is a catastrophe that has
only just begun:
*an interview with the author by
Teji Grover and Marietta
Taralrud Maddrell*

⊷⧭ ⧬⊶

Poems by Ingrid Storholmen
*English translation by
May-Brit Akerholt*

⊷⧭ ⧬⊶

TG: You are a poet who writes in the two Norwegian languages, Bokmål and Nynorsk, also experimenting by using these languages as two distinct poetic voices. How did the idea of writing a book about Chernobyl take hold of your imagination? You were twenty-four when you began working on the book, the pull of poetry must have been very strong, I imagine.

IS: Norway was heavily affected by the nuclear disaster. A lot of radioactive rain came to my hometown when I was a girl. Suddenly we could no longer eat blueberries and mushrooms, and as a child, I became very afraid of this invisible danger. Both my sisters fell ill in the years after Chernobyl. I felt I had to write this book on behalf of all the people affected by the tragedy.

In this book I have only used Bokmål, but in other books I use both languages. It feels like writing with both my hands. The two languages are quite similar, so the differences become rather important. The wealth of having two languages is very important to my writing. And the question of language has an interesting political history in Norway.

TG: You told me that your father is engaged in doing some research on the impact of radiation on the flora and fauna in your area? I believe he teaches science at the school called Vuku where he undertook this ambitious study.

IS: Perhaps quoting from Per Storholmen's project, *Radioactivity, Environment and Health* is in order here. You can first of all look at the map to take in the visual of the impact radioactivity had in large parts of Norway. It is a reconstruction of the spreading fallout from the catastrophe. Since 1986, my father has been diligently studying the amount of radioactivity present in the following: water, sediment, plankton, fish like trout and char; in mountain cranberry, mountain-cranberry soil; in the mushroom chantarelle, mushroom soil, cloud-berries, and blueberries. These have been tested every year in autumn since 1986 until the year 2011. The winter tests were done on the same fish, but also on trees like fir, juniper, pine, birch, alder, aspen, goat-willow. The berries that were tested included rowan and blueberries; lichen and the special lichen that reindeer feed on were also tested. Tests done in spring over the same period of time included trout, char, plankton and lichen.

As you can see for yourself, the levels of becquerel per kg are unpredictable over a passage of time and do not necessarily decline over the years. For instance the becquerel per kg in mushroom soil went up from 255 in 1986, soon after the disaster, to 2850 in 2010. So much for those who think the impact will thin out over a period of time. For the lichen that reindeer feed on, the levels became very high soon after the disaster. The level of becquerel in trout fish goes up a lot in winter, perhaps because the water is frozen.

TG: So you could say that your father's work on the subject was important to you when the idea of the book began to take hold of your imagination?

IS: Indeed it was important. The word 'becquerel' became a frequently used word when I was growing up: 'Ingrid, watch out, there's too much becquerel in the blueberries. Stay away from them.' When I became older, I realized what the word meant. When I began to write, the word and all its sinister implications engulfed me. My father had the facts, and I was going to have the fiction. Together, this might add up to quite a picture of the accident. The science and poetry of it all.

TG: Very recently, Ingrid, Mahua Majhi published a novel in Hindi about the devastating impact of uranium mining, in certain parts of India, on unsuspecting citizens as well as on the natural and social environment. This is perhaps the first of its kind in Hindi. Both of you should be able to read each other's work at some point of time. I have a feeling you have a lot to share with and learn from each other.

IS: I would love to read this book if it is published in English.

TG: You recently won the Sult Prize for your Chernobyl book. Do tell us a little about the significance of the prize, especially since it is named after the Nobel Prize winning author Knut Hamsun's epoch-making book *Hunger*. It's a rather unusual thing for a prize to be named after a specific work rather than the author. If you'd like to dwell on a few other Norwegian writers who won this prize before and after, it might afford a fuller glimpse into the way this prize works.

IS: This is a prize given to young writers in the beginning of their careers, and who have done something altogether different. It also recalls the travails of Hamsun's nameless hero in *Hunger*. It is also a big prize when it comes to money, so you do not need to go hungry for a long time afterwards... Among other writers who have won this prize, I can mention Gaute Heivoll,

Gunnhild Øyehaug, Carl Frode Tiller, Hanne Ørstavik and Ture Erik Lund – all very interesting fiction writers.

MM: How was your novel received in Norway?

IS: Very well indeed. I won five awards and prizes and received a three-year fellowship from the Norwegian government. The reviews were great! Many pointed out how important it is that we do not forget the disaster. They also noted the importance of writing poetically about a political subject. I have been reading from this novel at a number of literary events, but also in settings where environmental concerns are the agenda. I have been discussing the problems of using nuclear energy instead of clean energy produced by water, wind or sun. There is a sentence in my book, which, I think, summarizes my point of view: 'If a windmill turns over, it will not bring about changes in the genetic material of an embryo.'

TG: It might be in order here to share with you part of the ongoing debate about the issue in India. When it comes to setting up nuclear power projects in this country or giving green signals where decisions have been pending, there has been gross insensitivity. The government okayed the Jaitapur plant on the twenty-fifth anniversary of the Chernobyl disaster. One would have thought the recent catastrophe in Fukushima would have a sobering impact on the nuclear industry in India. Many countries are now following the 'pause and review' approach, but hurried and superficial internal reviews are conducted before the happy declarations of perfect safety make a mockery of the lessons we claim to have learnt from Fukushima. The protests in various parts of the country against proposed projects have been growing stronger, since the level of awareness about congenital deformities, cancer, and miscarriages has been constantly going up. This apart from the massive ecocide resulting from setting up 'plants', which are planted where real ones should have been allowed to stay.

IS: I'm acquainted with some aspects of the debate in India. I knew that lessons from Chernobyl could not possibly have been wasted either on the activists in India or people who would be affected by the power projects. I think painfully of the areas in India where the biodiversity 'hotspots' would make nuclear ventures seem unthinkable. But in what specific ways do you think the Chernobyl catastrophe enlightened people affected by the nuclear projects in India?

TG: I could give you one example, and the stories everywhere are similar, as you would know from your own experience. Villagers of Jaitapur, for instance, as pointed out by Praful Bidwai, are fairly knowledgeable about the impact of the Chernobyl disaster, things described so poetically and poignantly in your narrative, Ingrid. When many countries including Japan are entertaining serious doubt about the issue of nuclear power, India seems determined to let the industry flourish by buying reactors from countries that don't find ready market for their monstrous goods. I think your book has the potential of bringing poetry to corners that haven't had it so far.

IS: I hope so. There are countries that are going to try phasing out the use of nuclear power, though much remains to be seen what they eventually do with the waste. There are countries that could suffer by being the recipients of this waste.

TG: You have been to India a couple of times and visited places that interest you in much the same way as Chernobyl did. You visited the site of the worst industrial disaster in Bhopal and met the activists involved in running the wonderful healing place called the Sambhavna Trust Clinic. Your Chernobyl experience seems to have sensitized you to the human and environmental distress caused by those ventures of modern technology that lack foresight. Would you like to talk about your engagement with these issues that seems to spring from your deeply personal experiences?

IS: It meant a lot to me to visit Bhopal and meet the people there. They do a very important job, and the similarities to Chernobyl were very obvious. It is the same kind of disaster, and the same long-term problems and suffering. Another similarity between this accident and the one that took place in Bhopal in 1984 is that the American company responsible for the disaster took no responsibility whatsoever to help the victims. Nor did they help in cleaning up the sites. I hear that the toxic waste from the Union Carbide factory in Bhopal is still contaminating the drinking water supplies in the city. We saw the same indifferent attitude in the Soviet Union, to the extent that initially they didn't even admit that the disaster had taken place. In fact, Sweden informed the world about what had happened in Chernobyl. The people in Chernobyl are still waiting for help and support for their survival just as in Bhopal. What I wrote about Chernobyl in this book: Chernobyl is a catastrophe that has only just begun, seems to be equally true of Bhopal, if my impressions from a recent visit are anything to go by.

As I mentioned, both my sisters fell ill after being exposed to radioactive rain. And the farmers in my area still have to feed their sheep, cows and reindeer with clean food because the grass is still very poisonous. The same goes for fish, berries and mushrooms. From my father's research it is quite clear that the becquerel-levels in all these things are still very high.

My sisters' thyroid glands were damaged. Both of them have scars shaped like necklaces on their necks since they underwent surgery to have their glands removed. It's common knowledge that a thyroid disorder affects the metabolism, how warm and cold you feel, how energetic or tired you get and a lot of other things. It requires lifelong medication. At School No.6, which I visited near Kiev, many youngsters had scars like those of my sisters. The thyroid gland absorbs radioactivity. Iodine treatment might have helped, but the health authorities did not brief us about that. The schoolchildren in Ukraine did not get that sort of information either. I hear that the Union Carbide in Virginia did not care to inform the people in Bhopal about the antidote to MIC poisoning, some of whom might have been saved if they had simply used water.

It is important for me as a writer to use my voice to talk about this, so that people don't forget how dangerous radioactivity and the aftermath of a nuclear disaster can be. Fukushima is the most recent reminder for all of us, only if we're willing to heed it. I think that the future will judge us for using nuclear power and weapons.

TG: How do you manage to reconcile, at an artistic level, your poetic practice with your political engagement? I have in mind, in particular, your distinct preference for what you once described as 'intelligent metaphysical poetry'. It isn't hard to see in your Chernobyl book that your own poetry seems to have left a distinct mark on the way you write fiction. What would you say?

IS: The plot is not of prime importance to me. As a poet, I am more interested in situations, details, moments, and 'odd' uses of language. Even in my prose I try to use rhythm and metaphors and different kinds of language 'tools' to create a language that is far from the everyday language, or the language you find in official reports and in the newspapers. In this book, I wanted to create a language that could match the subject and hold the pain of the people from Chernobyl. I have tried to say things about people's feelings and fears – things that would never be heard in a reportage. I have tried to give the people of Chernobyl a voice that can be heard. I have tried to convey how afraid they are for themselves and their children and their future. I got to know a little about this after spending two months in the areas around the power plant, meeting people in hospitals, at schools and so on.

TG: A Norwegian critic said that if someone claims there are no political novels in contemporary Norwegian literature, then they should be hit on their heads with your novel. How do you view such comments, I mean when in your entire writing, the sheer joy of experimentation shines through, no matter what you might be writing, and howsoever dark the content might be?

IS: I like to use literary form as a part of the content. 'Who can tell the dancer from the dance…' But I also think that a big subject stirs up big thoughts. If you put people in a life and death situation, it will bring out the best and worst in the characters, and then you have to fuel a big fire. I did not try to write a political novel, but given the subject it is impossible for it not to be political. When you are using reality, and not a fictional disaster, political aspects will follow automatically.

TG: What you've just said might have a bearing on the novel you're writing at present. Is it all right for you to discuss your work in progress?

IS: The book I'm writing now is a novel about the Second World War and the German battleship Tirpitz, which was bombed and sunk in Tromsø in Northern Norway in 1944. There were about 2000 people on board, and only about 800 survived. Such a catastrophe has a lot of historical facts, like the name of the Royal Air Force bomber planes and the name of the bomb (Tallboy) and so on. I've done a lot of research and even went to Germany to meet the survivors from Tirpitz. Men who are now in their nineties, and who could tell a lot about the life on board, and also about the night on which the bombing took place. From there my own writing took off, and I see the ship as a mythological subject as much as a concrete battleship. And I imagine everything about the correspondence that might have taken place between these sailors and their girlfriends, their mothers and so on. Like in the Chernobyl book, here, too, there are people who tell their stories. From the Norwegian farmers living close to the site of the catastrophe to the British spies and German officers. Reading about all of this, my own imagination was set free.

Maybe I 'need' a huge catastrophe to write the kind of fiction I like. To put human beings in a situation of life and death – and see how they react. Who come out of it as heroes and who do not. To discuss love, faith and destiny based upon these special circumstances that a war creates. And there are always wars going on in the world, so this is not just about the Second World War but any war.

I think it's important for me to start with historical facts, to trigger me off. I've also done it in my third book of poems *Siriboka* (Siri's Book), which is about Siri, a woman who lived from 1800 to 1870. She is one of my ancestors who lived in the countryside where I was born. My most recent collection of poems *Til kjærlighetens pris* (To Praise Love) is about a trip that I made to the cave where Orpheus went to Hades to pick up his wife Eurydice on the border between Bulgaria and Greece.

TG: Would you like to comment on your fellow Norwegian writers in whose work the political does not compromise the artistic quality of the work? From among my own favourites, I could name Lars Amund Vaage's story 'Cows' that Hindi readers are now familiar with, Petterson's internationally acclaimed novel *Out Stealing Horses*, Edward Hoem's *Ave Eva*, all of which are profound meditations on what modernization has done to the human psyche and to the natural world.

IS: These men are a generation older than me, and they were all active on the literary scene in the political '70s. The Marxist literary project is very different from my more poetic entry into the subject, and in my book I do not mention politics at all, it is all between the lines. I think that the older generation has a more outspoken political intention. These men are great novelists and I think they have more or less given up the direct use of politics in their fiction in the recent years. Another important writer from Norway is Jon Fosse. He writes poetry, prose and essays, but it's his plays that have made him famous all over Europe, and after Ibsen, he is the most produced Norwegian playwright in Europe. His plays are very simple, and very, very beautiful. He is far from all politics in his work – all he writes is purely existential and poetic.

Tarjei Vesaas is no doubt the writer who has meant the most to me over the years, he is one of the best writers in Norway through all time, and one of his books, *Birds*, has just been translated into Hindi.

TG: You were planning to write a book about your travel in India. How far are you into it, if I may ask you? What might the content of this book be?

IS: I have written about 60 pages and also translated about 30 pages of Hindi poetry that will constitute an important part of the book. I will also focus on missionary history. Young people from Norway came to India to talk about God, but ended up working hard in the midst of the Santal-people for instance. I want to write about their lives and struggles, but also about the struggle of the Santals for a better life, a life that would be free of exploitation. I will also focus on my meeting with India, a meeting that changed my life and my way of thinking. Being in India was very spiritual for me, and has been very important later. It might sound like a cliché, but it is true. Meeting with poets from India has also been very interesting and gave me a lot to think about. It was the same, meeting people who had chosen a totally different kind of life, like walking around the river Narmada for three years, having come to India from other lands. I have been traveling all over, but India is the country that has changed me the most, and I am very happy that my book will be published there where I feel most touched by things.

MM: The episodic nature of your novel with its rapid shifts in perspective and voice fascinated me as a translator. Was it your intention to record the clamour of different voices as a metaphor for the fragmentation of their lives by the catastrophe?

IS: I have created a choir of voices to reflect that so many people were affected by the disaster. It was a challenge for me as a writer to try and understand many different people, to write about both men and women, young and old, worker and manager, rich and poor, educated and not educated, etcetera. I tried to find the language and points of view of all the different characters. I tried to portray how each one of them looks upon his/her destiny. Do they turn to God or away from God? Do they hate the government or themselves? Who do they blame? What do their fears and despair look like? What will their future be like?

I write about a seven-year-old boy who has terminal cancer and an old man who has to say goodbye to his apple trees before he is evacuated from his farm. We also meet a man high up in the communist party who takes his children and tries to escape to another country, and women who are afraid of having children with mutations and diseases due to radiation.

MM: One episode in the novel intrigued me a lot – the two silent sisters in the hall, cut off from their immediate outside world and possibly from the rest of the book. Will you tell us a little about how this section relates to Chernobyl?

IS: That is my little way of saying hello to the Russian writer Anton Chekhov and his three sisters in a famous play of his. It is also a way of showing how apathetic we humans can be in the time of a catastrophe, how we do not act even when we know that a disaster has taken place. I am very sorry for the people in the most affected areas of Belarus and Ukraine. They did not deserve a situation like this, being inflicted by the world's worst environmental accident that from one day to the other changed their lives forever. No one deserve this. It is time to put an end to this way of producing energy. There are over 400 nuclear power plants in the world; a new Chernobyl can happen anywhere, even in India.

MM: Your novel was published in Norway before the Fukushima disaster. In the light of your deep research into Chernobyl, how did you react to Fukushima?

IS: I thought it was terrible news from Japan, but not unexpected. Because of what I have seen when I went to Chernobyl, I have always felt it would happen again. And again. And then, it did happen again. I know how unsafe the power plants are. Fukushima showed us that nature can so easily destroy a man-made plant. Many of the power plants in Russia and other countries are very old and unsafe. An earthquake or even terrorism is a constant threat. A terrorist doesn't need atomic bombs. He can crash a plane into a power plant and cause another Hiroshima for free!

Another thing is that one should not ignore the possibility of human error that will trigger an accident. Nuclear power can be very, very dangerous, we know that, and therefore we need to start using some other kind of energy to save our planet.

MM: Are there any more questions you would have liked us to ask? For instance it might be interesting to know more about your life in the countryside in Norway. Your process of writing, the routines you follow, the high points of inspiration. Anything.

IS: I have been living in many places, both in Oslo, the capital of Norway, and in cities like Rome and Berlin. I really like being in a big city, but I do appreciate, more and more, a silent life near the forest and close to wild nature. Close to animals like elk and deer and foxes I can spot from my window. It has also become more and more important for me to spend time with my family. But it is also important for me to be able to travel a lot, all over the world. Travelling is necessary for my writing, and I often go away to write. Nothing beats a hotel room as a place for me to reach a deep focus and really come into my writing. I think concentration is more important than inspiration. And there are no distractions in a hotel room; I can just focus on the book, and do not even have to take care of my tea mug. If I am at home, I normally go to the library and sit there and work for some hours. I love sitting there, surrounded by the smell of books. That makes me feel less lonely, for writing is a very lonely job. Meeting good colleagues is important. No one else understands the process of making a book. While attending literary festivals, I meet other writers and can discuss literature, but in the end it is always good to go home and walk in the woods or look at a lake. There is a lot of poetry in nature, therefore it is so important that we take care of it.

A long time ago and quite soon could, can
this happen:
To be reached by love

Can you fold
me out
in
yes like a flower
like summer

The flowers are so different
You call me stories
there are great possibilities, I tell you

For all words are like you:
                    quivering
In our bodies truth

You stir in me
We shift the ground
                        the lair we lie in

When we cannot know whose stomach is
rumbling
it is closeness

I hold the face against my eye
with warm fingers
where is the simple hand
The lonely hand
The nerves in the hand are full-grown
My hand hurts, only you can heal it

When you are in your hand
The darkness of the palm
My hand is tired today
between the eye your arm

                        hands gather water-drops
                                    like gifts
the hands hold my name
the newborn name

                        The hands inside me, fingers fill me out

Holding hands
it is steep and wet
and we hold hands
with gloves and without

until the hands throw the gloves
                        skin
                                of lips thoughts touched

I take you   let you

be ablaze Fire
we might have said

but we grew utterly still
how still we become
when we talk, love
one heart in two

The rhythm of the morning heart
against a hand
you didn't wake from this

put me down there
so I can imagine the city alone

We delay the time
I wait by your side in the water
what is left of the night then
I should have left it a long time ago

until love
is able to touch
us
who cannot be touched

Something lets you know
Something which won't let go
You are not magic to me
We are everyday and don't like it
Friday, and it rains
It rains all day
An orange rain

I want to walk alone
It is spring, and it rains

I flee. Have already fled
You don't touch me, at least don't kiss me, I collapse
There is a bullet in the pistol, the roulette always wins
I collapse
from relief

All ages live in your face
the boy, the infant, the old, the strong, young
I watch you bend forwards
But you don't kiss me
1 out of 6 times you kiss me
Will you happen to kiss me now

I wait here
until you don't see me any longer
cut you up in such tiny pieces
that you exist everywhere
I can lose you   like that
                can I lose you

You exist side by side
and you